Monika Maron

THE DEFECTOR

translated by

David Newton Marinelli

readers international

The title of this book in German is *Die Überläuferin*, first
published in 1986 in West Germany by S. Fischer Verlag
GmbH, Frankfurt am Main.

Copyright © 1986 S. Fischer Verlag GmbH, Frankfurt am
Main

First published in English by Readers International Inc. and
Readers International, London. Editorial inquiries to London
office at 8 Strathray Gardens, London NW3 4NY England.
US/Canadian inquiries to Subscriber Service Department,
P.O. Box 959, Columbia LA 71418-0959 USA.

English translation copyright © 1988 Readers International

Cover art and design by Jan Brychta
Typesetting by Grassroots Typeset, London N3
Printed and bound in Great Britain by Richard Clay Ltd,
Bungay, Suffolk

British Library Cataloguing in Publication Data
Maron, Monika
    The defector
    I. Title II. Die Überläuferin. *English* 833'.914 [F]
                                            PT2673.A4686

ISBN 0-930523-40-7 hardback
ISBN 0-930523-41-5 paperback

For the third time it was night. The moon danced on an invisible rope from one side of the street to the other. It needed two hours to cross; she knew that from previous nights. For two days she had been lying, sitting in bed, on the rug, in the chair, and she was surprised that she had not felt hunger or thirst in two days, nor a need to use the toilet. She hadn't slept in fifty-four hours and she wasn't tired now either. If anything, she had had a rather insatiable need for sleep in the last few years, which intensified to a virtual addiction during the winter months. But she was less astonished at her constantly alert senses than at the general absence of bodily wants. Her body seemed to be carrying out all vital functions without asking for anything in return. Even the thought of larded saddle of venison with morel sauce could not arouse hunger, or even appetite. She could not explain her condition to herself and simply hoped that it would last without her having to waste away to skin and bones, because it saved her from otherwise insurmountable obstacles. As things were, no one had to shop or cook for her, and most important, she needed very little money. And it almost seemed as though she could count on these happy circumstances because she felt strong and healthy, apart from her legs, which had lost all feeling. Perhaps her body had finally understood what had been expected of it for so long. It had always consoled her with alms: tonsils, gall bladder, even a kidney. But freedom never lasted more than a few weeks, at most months. It had now finally understood, Rosalind thought, that the wretched little organs it was willing to sacrifice were not enough to be discharged from the lifelong obligation to work.

One of the odd things that had happened to her during the last three days was that her telephone hadn't rung even once. There weren't many people who Rosalind could assume would miss her after a few days. One of them, however, was obliged to notice her absence: Siegfried Barabas, chairman of that institute for historical research to which Rosalind had been assigned fifteen years ago as a university graduate and where, except for weekends, national holidays, vacations or when illness allowed her, she had to show up every day at 7:45 am and stay until 5:00 pm.

Every day at 7:05 the same path through the small shady street in which she lived, down to Becherstrasse, formerly Breite Strasse (street names are rather like women's—they are born, married, divorced, reborn, according to which men or governments they happen to belong to). Fifty yards west along Becherstrasse up to the stop for the No. 46 tram in the direction of Kupfergraben, a thirty-minute ride up to the Weidendamm Bridge, down Schiffbauerdamm next to the River Spree barricaded with a high wall of corrugated metal. They installed the sheets two years ago. Rosalind could observe from her office how the river gradually disappeared behind the grey metal sheets, put up no doubt to protect it from diving escapees or from the temptation to imitate the free flight of the seagulls, who moved, in search of food, unconcerned between the Bode Museum and Lützowufer. Along Schiffbauerdamm past Albrechtstrasse, underneath the suburban train bridge which carries the trains to the West, into the next millenium for her as well, if she doesn't die beforehand. Just a few steps more to the narrow grey building upon which a cast-iron plate next to the main door proclaims it the most important scholarly institution in the country. Past the porter, a friendly man despite the reputation of his profession, who was unable to continue working as a railroad engineer due to an accident in which he lost his right leg. Now he looked out of the porter's lodge the way he used to in his locomotive, with one arm resting at a right angle over the wooden frame, his eyelids slightly pressed together as if he had to fight a headwind. Two floors higher, across the smoothly polished linoleum floor already frayed at the edges, and Mrs Petri's reproving look at being five minutes late, Barabas' renewed request for changes in her last paper. Then her room, nine square yards, sunless until 4:00 pm, journals, catalogue cards, the boarded-up Spree, her typewriter, the customs officials on their way to work, from work, the dogs which they say are addicted to blood and drugs—and this, every day.

Usually Barabas had sick employees phoned after half a day in order to obtain an excuse for unauthorized absence from their place of work, and it was inconceivable that he would forego this information in her case. But she didn't want to think of Barabas now. What was happening to her just now was too marvelous for her to want to mix it up with the deadly dull banalities of the day-to-day life she had just fled. Perhaps the Barabas institution had burned down, and she had since been listed as a trapped victim of the catastrophe, or they had simply forgotten she existed. Barabas

3

had opened the padded door to his room on Tuesday thinking over which of his employees he wanted to call to him at 7:45, and wasn't able to think of Rosalind because she had been deleted from his memory like a program from a computer.

After Rosalind had become convinced her condition was a lasting one, she began to think about how she should use the expanse of time she suddenly had at her disposal. Her first thoughts were directed toward classifying the time, but that depended on what she wanted to do with it; was it to be apportioned this way or that until she had used it up, or was it a space to be filled with occurrences and thoughts? She found it difficult to decide between these two attitudes, which were hostile, or so she thought, one to the other. She liked the profligate and generous character of the first; it also fit in with the need she now had of doing without things. At the same time, however, it seemed frivolous to her that a person in her situation should want to leave to oblivion the only thing she owned: an abundance of time, like a tree abandoning its withered leaves to the autumn wind. It made more sense, she thought, to look at time as a restricted space in which she wanted to collect experiences like books in a library, memories accessible to her all the time. A unique possibility not to have to leave anything behind again, never again to have to leave one time for another. From now on she would remain while she went away, and depart while she stayed. She could also recall times past in this room and fuse desired future time to a lasting present. An unending orgy of fantastical events was at hand, a marvelous chaos with no fixed purpose, in so far as the familiar order of her brain permitted.

Let me begin then with the first catastrophe of my life, the cause of all those that followed, none of which can compare in tragedy and greatness with the first. Only the last, my death, will, I hope, be the equal of the first: my birth.

My mother and I had spent the last night before my birth in the hospital. I did not wish to be born and kept still. My mother, however—I clearly felt this—wanted to get rid of me. The others as well—to judge from their gruff voices, which I can remember exactly, it must have been the nurses—asked every half hour if it was time yet, if I had finally begun to make my way into the world. My mother pressed and pushed me with her muscles so that I was shoved back and forth, as a result of which I have retained a decided dislike, almost a phobia, against every kind of pushing and shoving. I was suddenly startled because my mother had had a violent start, and the sound of the siren, which I already knew, penetrated to me muted by the membrane of the womb. My mother traded her place in bed for one underneath it. We crouched on the floor, and my mother finally stopped using her muscles against me. I was sorry for her because she was trembling so, which made the water I was squatting in splash in tiny waves; that felt pleasant. Later on as well, in my basinette, I liked this kind of waves. My gentle delight ended as bombs exploded to the left and right of us. My young mother, younger than I was ever to know her again, wept and moaned at the same time as I was hoping to die like this in her womb, and to avoid a cold, painful death on my own. But my mother seemed to want the exact opposite. Right after the bombs fell she began her hostile pushing again, more violently than before, such that the membrane burst and my vital water flowed away. My mother, still crouched under the bed, cried out for the nurses. Too young and inexperienced, she was terrified by the water. The nurses came to the bed, but did not find us, and they could not see in the air raid blackout. Here, my mother whimpered. She had begun to be overcome by contractions so strong that she could hardly move—here I am. The nurses dragged us out from under the bed, scolding, and threw us on top of it again. Having lost the least desire to be born, I considered what I could do now, at such an advanced stage, to prevent it. I wrapped the umbilical cord around my neck, hoping this would strangle me as my mother expelled me. But when I was caught in the whirlpool, the cord slipped off, and I did not have the strength to repeat the whole procedure. Once outside I was dazzled by the darkness into which I was born, almost to blindness, as the sirens screeched all-clear over the remains of the city, so deafening that I hear them to this day when it is very quiet. I yelled for help as loud as I could. But not even my mother understood why I was crying. And had she understood she wouldn't have put me back in her womb anyway. I didn't forgive her for six weeks. It was only then that I opened my eyes and looked at her for the first time.

*

Apart from a deficient will to live, the circumstances of my birth left me with two things: a barren body and an interest in death that aroused the astonishment of those around me while I was still a child. Up until his death six years ago, my father accused me of wishing to kill him when I was four, as I insisted almost every day on burying him with a dustpan and brush. Having been in the war and a prisoner of war camp, he had no use for such games, although he surely would have forgiven me if his feelings for me had not been

6

troubled by the doubt as to whether I was really the fruit of his seed. Later, when a hereditary eye defect of his family showed up in me, all doubt was eliminated, but I was already six years old at the time, and he had forgotten how to love me. I don't remember the real reason I had for burying my father every day. I don't believe that I wanted his absence, because I was glad to be one of those children who had a father. At the time, death was an everyday matter. Everyone spoke about the dead as they did about the living, what they said, whose parents or children they were, how they went with them to the movies. Uncle Paul was dead, my grandparents were dead, the daughter of the merchant Kupitzki was dead because she wanted to save the bales of material from the burning building, Aunt Lotte died after she was told that her son had been killed in action. Through photos and stories I had such a clear picture of all the dead as if I had known them and they had just gone away on a trip. I was allowed to place lily of the valley on the grave of Aunt Lotte, whom I had actually known, because they were her favorite flowers and, as my mother said, she would like them. Those who could enjoy themselves lived on, although they were as invisible as air. I would never have thought of letting a child die in my play. Only grownups had a right to die, and only they knew what it meant. My father had to let his hand hang limp over the chair arm and wasn't allowed to tighten it when I swung it. It had to remain without feeling until I had buried it, and wake up as soon as I commanded it. Be dead, wake up, be dead, wake up, like Snow White and Sleeping Beauty. I think this game comforted me; the comfort lay in the revocability of death, which I hoped for just as I had hoped before birth for my life to be rescinded. I wanted the resurrection of all the dead I had seen; to have the memory of them turn out to be a correctable error, so that I could forget them, the many dead on a Sunday in February, when we, my mother and I, were looking for Ida in the rubble of the Neander Quarter. My mother wore her black coat of pony fur which my father had sent her from Paris, and she had painted her beautiful lips blood red, probably because it was Sunday. So we took the subway to the Neander Quarter where Ida lived and which, as we had heard on the radio, had been bombed the day before. In the subway tunnel a nauseating smell surged toward us. Outside a cold dusty smoke hung over the collapsed buildings, which made me sick and my eyes water. Sitting on my mother's arm with my face buried in the smooth black fur of her coat, I didn't see the first corpses we walked over. It wasn't until I noticed my mother's body tremble and her sobbing that I looked over her shoulder at the lifeless, twisted bodies below us partially covered by the rubble. My mother's weeping upset me more than the corpses. Ida would cry, I would cry, but Mother did not cry, at least not when I was around to see her. It wasn't until eight years later that I heard her cry, for the second time. She was kneeling down in front of the open kitchen cupboard to get out the coffee when the great Russian funeral march *Immortal Sacrifice* was played on the radio. Generalissimo Stalin had died. I was ashamed that I didn't have to cry like my mother and didn't ask her until the next day if it was all right to wear rollerskates during the period of national mourning. My mother walked carefully over the bodies in her boots with the high heels so as not to stumble and fall between them. Ida's building didn't exist anymore, all that was left was a pile of rose-colored stones on top of furniture and other scraps of the living from which, here and there, the arms and legs of buried people stuck out. My mother wept, and her tears

8

ran over her mouth and mixed with the lipstick to form little rivulets that flowed from the corners like blood. Wotcha bawlin for, at least ya can paint ya lips agin, them 'ere can't, a man called out who was collecting the bodies from the street and piling them up against the intact wall of a building. Her sobs became more violent, so that she could hardly see through her tears, and we almost tripped over the legs of the dead woman. Ida is dead, Ida is dead, my mother wailed, looking among the many feet for the red ski boots that Ida always wore during air raids, so that she would have something warm on her feet if she were bombed out. We didn't find Ida's red ski boots, nor did we find Ida. Three days later she was standing at our door after they had treated her for smoke poisoning at the hospital. Ida was alive, Ida was not dead, Ida almost died. It was a miracle that she was still alive, Ida said. My mother said Ida was a borderline case between life and death. Later on, we forgot about that and got used to Ida's life having been spared, until she died more than thirty years later—then I remembered that there would almost have been no Ida in my life. Later on, when I sought my own acquaintance with death, without the mediation of grownups, the great temptation was to stand at the brink without crossing it. In a winter's night, dressed only in a nightgown, crouched on the balcony and waiting to see if fatal pneumonia would attack me; on the subway stop pushing and flexing my toes over the edge of the platform as the train arrived. I've devised my own death a hundred times in order to punish my parents.

When I was thirteen I had to have my appendix out. Two days before I went to the hospital, I told my parents at dinner that I was afraid of the operation. My mother calmed me down by saying it was a minor operation in which nothing could happen to me.

How d'you know, my father said, slurping the bean soup—green beans with beef—plenty a people die in these operations.

He wants me to die, I thought.

My mother kept still.

My father continued slurping.

When I had to fetch a beer for him from the kitchen I heard my mother say: Do you have to scare her like that, Herbert?

I opened the bottle in the kitchen and spat into the beer.

I gave up the idea of punishing my parents with my death. From then on I wanted my father to die. I never had the thought in exactly these words, I simply wanted him to disappear. He should go away, I thought; I left the rest to a just fate for which I was not responsible. He lived another twenty years. When he died I felt for the first time the painful sensation that death was irrevocable. As they carried him out of the house, I held open the double swinging doors, one door with each arm, so that the bearers had to duck under. As they struggled to manoeuvre the bier with the corpse through the barrier that I of all people had become on his last passage out of this house, one of his cold, rigid limbs brushed me. He had died sitting, and for that reason, as *rigor mortis* had not yet ceased, he lay on the bier with bent and outstretched arms and legs. He looked like a slaughtered animal which had been hung over a pole with its fore and hind legs tied together. The men had wrapped him in white cloths held together with safety pins. In a number of places the cloths did not quite meet, and bare skin, colored pink by *livor mortis*, was visible. I walked behind them up to the garden gate, followed them to the street, watched as they manoeuvered him into the car, which was grey and not otherwise identifiable as a hearse. The men said goodbye with silent, serious nods. As they got into the driver's cab I noticed that the driver's mate turned on the radio. I walked to the middle of the roadway and looked after them until they turned onto the main street. Then I was certain: he was gone. I went back into the house, slowly, looking at the changes, with an unbelieving eye. He won't walk this path anymore, he planted the roses but I'll see them; the house belonged to him but I will be inside it. My mother is weeping over him and I will comfort her. I have won, I thought. I was left with the satisfaction, the shame of it and the certainty that things would remain the way they were now once and for all; there was no way to mitigate them, the answer had not been given and was now impossible. I had wanted to love him until yesterday; today he was dead.

The fact that I could not punish my father through my death, that I punished him instead by living, that I was a living punishment for the one who had begot me, did not diminish my innate interest in death. The older I became the more urgently I sought to be close to it; without it I felt defenseless and helpless. It was my guarantee against unbearable sadness or bodily pain. I sometimes met death. We would meet by a lake, in the woods or at my house. He would come in various shapes, as a gentleman in elegant clothes, as a hairy ruffian, he even came as a woman. I dallied with him, lay down next to him naked and offered myself to him. He would not take me. He knew what I was up to and that I would jump up at the last instant and run away. He would, however, reveal himself. When he revealed himself it would be too late for me to recognize him. He would smile at me with a pale pink human mouth in the face of a dog, get up on his hind legs, put his paws heavily on my shoulders and dance with me as I buried my hands deep in his fur and sought protection from him as I had sought it in my mother's lap from her blows, or later, as I sought protection on men's shoulders from their dissecting eyes. We danced in wild circles until the rhythm of my heart was like a drum roll and the dizzying blur of colors threw me off balance. It wasn't until I had awoken from my fainting spell that I would recognize him. The first time, he appeared to me as my own death.

The last time I met him was on Ida's bed. A cool sunny day in September. I had bought thirty red roses at the market with the last money I had.

'At's a proper bouquet, 'at is, the vendor said.

It's for someone who's dying, I said.

Well, ya don't say, the man replied.

Ida lay alone in bed in a white room; a tube ran from somewhere under her covers into a glass container. Ida gave a rattle in her death throes, every breath seemed to take her last bit of strength and pain. I put the flowers into a urinal that the nurse gave me for this purpose, on the console in front of the mirror, so they would be doubled and so Ida, in case she opened her eyes again, could see them.

Ida's breathing didn't sound human, more like the pounding of a machine. I took her hand; it was hot. Ida, I said; maybe she heard me. After a while I placed the roses in front of the window so I could see them when I wanted to escape for a few seconds the sight of Ida's face with the caked opening that was her mouth. At one point the door behind my back opened quietly, and the nurse stuck her head through the crack to see whether Ida was done yet with dying. Why can't she simply stop breathing, I thought, why does a person have to breathe when all it does is torment them? Don't exert yourself so, I said to Ida and stroked her arm, don't be afraid and don't contradict him, he's always right in the end. She must have heard me because her hand grew slowly cooler and her breathing calmer. Then we were alone in the room, he and I, and I saw him finally, gently, draw Ida into himself, while Ida's lungs gave up the struggle and were satisfied with what they received without exertion, until Ida was hardly breathing anymore—just now and then—and I thought every breath was her last. One of them was: a relieved exhalation, nothing more. It's true, I thought, a human being breathes her last.

The nurse asked whether I wanted to take Ida's things with me right then, because of the lack of space. The last color had already left Ida. That too was true, the waxen hue of the dead. It wasn't until I asked whether there was some place I could smoke a cigarette that the nurse looked at me and led me out of the room by the elbow. When I came back five minutes later they had driven off with Ida. The nurse said she put three roses on the bed.

That was my last encounter with him.

Rosalind interrupted herself, first, because a drowsy fly was buzzing around her room in aimless dives, distracting her with its insistent, monotonous humming, and second, because her thoughts—though she had put as much distance between them and her point of departure as possible—kept narrowing on fewer and fewer people, and if she were to continue pursuing them as before, she would soon find herself faced with the question of why she was alive in the first place. Rosalind had no answer to the question, as she knew from earlier efforts to discover one. She was living because she hadn't died—and so lived happily ever after, like the fairy tale. She decided not to come any closer to the question.

She was crouched in her chair. Behind the window, dawn

timidly separated the grey contours of the buildings opposite from the darkness. The new day concerned her as little as all the new days that would follow. She was free now, she said that to herself over and over; nevertheless, her thoughts ended in the same questions they had always ended in before. How could she learn a new way of thinking this quickly? she wondered. Paths of thought are like streets, paved with cobblestones or concrete, one went along them as usual, unawares; at best one sought a turning one hadn't noticed before, or beat a small path to the left or right into the unknown. Her articulated system of main and secondary streets, alleys, and trails, quite adequate for her life up until now, turned out to be a trap for every one of her thoughts. In this way, Rosalind thought, all present and future would produce nothing more than the constant repetition of the past, which would only bore and not assist her. She needed secret tracks, hidden paths, subterranean passageways and mountain ridges. She had once known such paths. Once, that was one of those words; Ida, tell me something that happened once; fairy tales begin with *once*. Once was not so far in the past as Onceuponatime, but it wasn't the day before yesterday either. In the time, therefore, between onceuponatime and the day before yesterday Rosalind's thoughts had travelled mysterious paths, almost as mysterious as Martha's thoughts. Except that Martha also knew paths through the air, ones Rosalind had never found.

I met Martha one summer fifteen years ago. The city was utterly empty. I didn't have the vaguest idea where to go on vacation and had stayed at home. I sometimes went to the café near my apartment in the evening in the hope of meeting someone I knew after all. Every time I came in, I saw a young woman sitting at one of the tables off to one side. Although she was strikingly beautiful she always sat alone. She was delicately built, had dark eyes half concealed by heavy eyelids, and almost black hair. Because of her foreign appearance and loneliness I called her the Stranger.

At times I thought I heard a hurried, incomprehensible whispering from the girl's direction. I would have liked to talk to her: Hello, who are you and why are you so alone? But I didn't dare. The uncertain fear of crossing a boundary or of breaking a secret law held me back. And none of the other guests broke through the Stranger's loneliness, so I wasn't able to find out whether the Stranger wanted to be alone or whether she was condemned to be.

I once had a dream about her. We were sitting in a restaurant that resembled a supermarket but there was a swimming pool in the middle of it. The Stranger and I sat across from each other and smiled. I'd like to have coffee, too, the Stranger said. When the waiter came with the coffee she had disappeared. I found her in the pool, where she was swimming in circles, smiling all the while. After that she came back to the table. Once again we sat silent across from each other until I asked: What is your name? The Stranger smiled nervously. Yes, indeed, she said, stood up and went toward the swimming pool. The moment I wanted to start a conversation with her, she got up quietly and disappeared into the green water. After the third attempt she didn't come back. I looked for her among the tables and the swimmers. She didn't turn up.

After that dream I decided to accost her. I was afraid that the dream might have a meaning and that the Stranger would one day dissolve into memory, and I would never find out who she was or why I felt so akin to her.

That evening I sat down at her table without asking whether she minded or not.

Good evening, I said.

Good evening, she said, without looking at me.

My name is Rosalind.

The Stranger raised her head. I don't know you, she said.

I had a dream about you, I said.

She looked at me with curiosity. It's nice not knowing you. I know most people here.

Then why are you always alone?

She looked me over as though she had to decide first whether to tell such an important piece of information. At the same time she traced the lines in her left palm with her right index finger.

I don't like to talk anymore, she said and drew the last word out so long that you could tell the sentence wasn't finished.

Why not? I asked.

She hesitated again, looked alternately at my hands and eyes. You are asking me all the wrong questions, she said. Everyone asks something and everyone asks the wrong things.

And what is the right question?

I don't know yet, but when someone asks it I'll recognize it.

I don't know it either, I said.

That doesn't matter, she said. As long as we don't know each other, the wrong questions aren't so boring.

We drank wine.

Why do you come here if you don't want to talk?

For the first time she laughed, a sniggering, secretive laugh. Sometimes strangers come, she said. I talk with them. Only strangers can know what I want to know. I don't know why, but sometime or other one of them will ask the right question

Some say I'm crazy, do you think so?

I don't know, I said, what if you were? I read that in a crazy world, insanity is the highest sanity.

Goodness gracious Hölderlin, so we end up in the looney bin! the Stranger said and laughed again her sniggering, conspiratorial laugh.

She exuded a sort of seduction, though I wouldn't have known how I felt seduced and to what. It was the seduction of a poem I didn't understand, but whose melody and resonances touched me all the same; or of music that brought strangeness into my own flesh.

Do you know who my father was? she said. She whispered and looked around at the next tables, from which, now and again, came attentive glances. My father is the secret king of the Jews, she said. Many, many years ago he was called to Spain on a secret matter. He didn't return. They said he got lost and can't find the way back. I say they're holding him prisoner.

And your mother? I asked.

My mother died when she was a child, she was nine or ten; I was delivered by someone else. When she visits she drags me to the mirror and points out how much we look alike. She screeches the same thing every time: you see, the eyes, this mouth, this chin, look like they're cut from the same face. I can't recognize anything; everyone has eyes, mouth and chin. She wants to be my mother, God only knows why. I don't like her.

There must be something to being a mother, I said, they're all like that, it ennobles them. They feel like slave and slave-keeper at the same time, that's what they call maternal love.

I didn't go on. Lost in thought, the Stranger traced the lines in her right palm, as if she wanted to change their course violently. She didn't seem to pay attention.

My name is Martha, she said in a whisper, with an imploring look, which left the impression that I had just been party to a great secret. She calls me Barbie, that's the name she baptized me with, she claims, but my name's Martha.

The waiter placed the bill on the table without a word. It was ten in the evening and the café was closing.

I know that's not how it was the first time I met Martha, although I can't imagine how it could have been any different. It wasn't like that, and yet that is how things continued that evening between Martha and me. We walked through the quiet streets lit by harsh streetlights, and it seemed to me that this nocturnal moment inserted itself over the earlier time like one layer of earth over another. I suddenly thought that I had run into Martha too, or someone who looked like her at another place, as she walked next to me with firm steps and her back upright, lending her an odd air of determination. This is where I went to school, Martha said, pointing into the darkness of a side street.

That Martha had gone to school, as I had, seemed strange to me. I would have thought up another childhood for Martha. A ruined castle was part of it, at least a woodland or lakeside cottage, and instead of teachers paid by the state, I would have given her a governess who told fairy tales.

Why do all children go to school every morning? Martha said. They trudge along their hated way like lambs, and wish the school had turned into a smouldering heap of rubble overnight because someone finally took the effort to set it on fire. But they all go. Probably everyone goes because the others do.

They could get a conspiracy together, I said.

And evenings they have to return to their slave-keepers,

one by one.

They could stay together, in groups of five or ten, I said.

All the same, Martha said, for each child there are two grownups, father and mother.

We walked along a small and (as far as one could see in the dark) well-cared-for front yard.

I live on the ground floor, Martha said.

I had expected something completely different. Not that I had any particular notion of what Martha's apartment would look like, but I had imagined a less exclusive neighborhood, a less orderly building: even the front door was locked.

Maybe Georg is still awake, Martha said.

Who is Georg?

My husband, Martha said.

I remember the hurt these two words inflicted at the time, the physical pain that pierced me and took my breath away. Up until then Martha had seemed to me the loneliest of mortals, and, although I didn't admit it to myself, nor even think about it, I had tied the vague hope to Martha's loneliness that we would—only perhaps and not right away, you know, gradually—form an alliance. Her loneliness seemed to me to be a guarantee that we would keep a certain distance from each other, because it was apparent that Martha was not inclined to fuse her life frivolously with someone else's. But she was a wife with a husband.

First Interlude

At this moment Rosalind heard from the rear corner of her room, as yet still quite dark in the dawn, hissing voices and the scraping sounds of feet and chair legs. She looked cautiously over the back of her chair and recognized a square table lit by candle light around which a number of figures were assembled: men, then two women as well; she thought she knew them all, though she was unable to remember either their names or how she had made their acquaintances. Hello, Rosalind said, how did you get in here? What do you want? I live here. Either the figures couldn't hear or they acted as if they didn't.

Hey, Rosalind called.

When once again the strangers didn't respond, all she could do was watch them quietly, hidden by the back of her chair, to wait and see what they were planning.

They raise their glasses and nod to one another.

The woman with the high voice:

> To our hostess, who has gone to such trouble.

The man in the red uniform:

> Where is our hostess, the proper thing would be to greet us.

The man with the bloody nose:

> Yes, where is the hostess, this is really…

In mid-sentence the man stops, frightened, pulls his head back in resignation and presses a handkerchief to his nose, which has begun to bleed again.

The woman with a mind of her own:

> If I may be allowed to express an opinion, I find it rather impolite.

She follows her sentence with a quiet, elegant cough.

The man with the unhappy childhood says nothing, he is sitting with his knees pressed together and his back straight as a ramrod. He is thinking about something, presumably sad.

The man in the red uniform:

> I suggest that we begin without her.

The woman with a mind of her own:

That's what I think.

The woman with the high voice:

Oh yes, what a wonderful idea, one must be strong, too.

The man with the unhappy childhood:

Have I already told you that I had a very unhappy childhood?

The man in the red uniform raps his knuckles on the table:

The discussion will take place later. Let's look at the agenda. Point one: order and law. Point two: law and order. Point three: aw and loder. The utmost priority for us firefighters. The demands of the moment. Each and every gallon of water for putting out fires flows for peace. Citizens, support your fire department in their fight for peace. Only things that burn can be extinguished. Volunteer as arsonists' assistants. Set your houses on fire.

The woman with a mind of her own:

If you want to know my opinion, you shouldn't ask people to do that kind of thing. It's totally irrational: set your houses on fire. Set fire to houses, now that's a different story, and you'll find people to help you. That's the whole point, isn't it?

The woman with the high voice drains her glass in a single draught, spilling half of it in the process because her hands are trembling with excitement:

Oh, am I confused. The very thought of it: the glare of the fire in the night sky. But are we concerned here with the beautiful, and the good? When they marched through our city back then, Mommy pulled the curtains shut and said: we're not going to look at that, child. And where was the lovely streaming sunlight, locked out by the cur-

tains on that most splendid of all days in May? But Mommy was such a strong person.
The man with the bloody nose:

No, stop, that's enough. I'm sorry: I'm awfully sorry, but if I go on listening to much more of this I run the risk of a hemorrhage, and no one can expect me to want that. The role of firefighting is dealt with exhaustively in Marx, I refer you to the Green Edition, beginning on page one hundred ninety-eight thousand three hundred forty-three. There is an explicit warning against overestimating the fire extinguishing authorities which, as Marx rightly predicts, must stop, given the inherent nature of firefighting, at the incitement to pyromania.

The woman with a mind of her own:

I see. Is that supposed to mean that they're not supposed to put it out? That's anarchy. It has to be extinguished. Try setting your house on fire and then stand idly by as it burns to the ground when no one comes to put it out. Like to see if you're against extinguishing then. Overestimating, hah, like to know what you mean by that.

The man with the unhappy childhood:

Oh, please, can't you change the subject. I had to do eight hours of homework every day, and I would have been glad if the fire department had come to enforce a break, but until I was nineteen my mother refused to let me touch matches. I'm forty now. Do you know that I can't laugh?

He pulls the corners of his mouth apart with his fingertips, and when he lets go, his lips come together and re-shape the small, hanging mouth under his moustache.

You see, I can't do it. You have to learn to laugh when

you're a child, and I had a very unhappy childhood, which, as we know, is the same as having no childhood at all.

Could you please be so kind as to talk about laughter? The woman with the high voice takes off her glasses, pulls a handkerchief with pale violet crocheted edges from her pocket. She begins to weep:

Oh, how awful.

The man in the red uniform:

The agenda! We railroad men like to laugh, too, but the prerequisite for laughter, I must emphasize, for all laughter, is law and order. Man, howwonderfulthatsounds, is not born to laugh but to live a meaningful life, we railroad men were born to run the railroad, that is why the railroad was invented. You can read that in Marx on page eighty-six thousand seven hundred thirty-seven in the Yellow Edition, yes indeed, and I reject the objection you are just about to raise. Keep quiet or I'll report you to your department, or don't you have a department, don't you have any meaning at all in your life?

The man with the bloody nose carefully blows out the air which he has been collecting in his lungs in order to contradict, when a rivulet of bright red blood begins to flow from his nose:

I beg your pardon, but it's a disease. If I don't say certain sentences it starts to bleed. I've already been to several doctors on account of it.

The man in the red uniform:

Very interesting. And which sentences are you talking about?

The man with the bloody nose keeps still, which makes his nosebleed worse.

The man with the unhappy childhood whispers:

…not born to laugh, not born to laugh, is born not to laugh. That sounds blasphemous. I am a professor of mathematics and am sixty years old, because they stole twenty years from me, and twenty stolen years are twenty years less until my death. And then I'll die for not having laughed, this is inhuman, believe me, you forget the most important things—I unfortunately don't know the exact term for it—not having been given to me as a whole. It's nothingness in me, assuming there was anything at all.

The woman with a mind of her own:

A professor and he talks such a load of nonsense, abuses his own mother. She stole twenty years. She gave you your entire life, he doesn't say that, stolen, he says, about his own mother. And he himself admits that he's a nobody, a nobody unfit to live. I'm a mother myself; I know what I'm talking about.

The man in the red uniform:

To the agenda! The agenda! We postal employees demand security. We do not want to be the cesspool of society. Stolen money, falsified love letters, probably full of spelling mistakes, divorce proceedings, thoughts dangerous to the state, we have to touch all of this filth with our own hands. We are forced to serve criminals and deliver money to whores. A whole profession is in danger of moral decay. Not to mention the hazard to life and health from infection. We demand the abolition of the delivery regulations. Down with sealed letters! Down with the compulsory delivery of letters! Up with health screening for mail users! Long live the free postal employee!

The woman with the high voice is still weeping:

Well, what can I say, most of all, what should I cry about, it's all so terrible. These poor postal employees, how well I can understand them, all that muck every day. But the poor bad people, are they to remain forever without news of the good, left to their wickedness? And the poor children. Oh, how ecstatic I am for every hello. And what about Christmas when the packages arrive? Mommy always said: children, think of lasting values as well.

The woman with a mind of her own:

Aha, that's going too far for me. You have to have a mind of your own, not a little here and a little there, you have to have an unequivocal mind of your own. I have the opinion of the postal employee because I'm opposed to everything criminal.

The man with the bloody nose suffers the feared hemorrhage. Frothy blood gushes out of his nose and mouth, squirts onto his white handkerchief and onto the clothes of those sitting around him, who now, except for the man in the red uniform, all look like butchers or surgeons.

The man in the red uniform:

I am imposing a state of emergency! Arrest the hostess!

The others jump up from their seats and begin to search the room:

Yes, where is the hostess? Where is she hiding? We have to find her. We want to arrest her.

After a few moments of uncertainty I decided to believe my eyes. I eagerly followed the spectacle before me, my attention distracted only by a high-spirited joy aroused by my wonderful new ability. A sober delirium, reasonable madness, dream without sleep. They played and played while I imagined whom I would invite in the future to this inner theater I had just created. Anyone, everyone, whether I knew them or not, I could have everyone dance and talk before me, even the Pope, if I felt like it. I didn't admit any doubts that I could repeat this or a similar vision. Doubts would have impeded my powers of imagination. Already utterly absorbed in plans for visions to come, I had almost forgotten to limit the impertinence of my guests. The man in the red uniform had just discovered me behind my chair back and rushed toward me with his heavy black boots, a triumphal twinkle in his eyes.

I've got her, I've got her, he screamed.

Stop, I called, not softly, but not loudly either. He had to stop in his tracks.

I said: Apart from your shameful attack on me, I agree to the form of association between you and me which you just tested out. For the duration of my interest I grant you freedom of thought and the right to free speech. Acts of violence against me, your hostess, are strictly prohibited under penalty of being forgotten. Please go now, and don't come again until I call you.

They left the room, one after the other; only the unhappy man remained standing in the doorway, undecided.

I am truly sorry, he said, I was unacquainted with the ladies and gentlemen. I do not understand how I got into their company.

That may have been my mistake, I said. I will be inviting you again soon to another scene. The man nodded a thank you and walked backward through the door, which he closed silently behind him. To make sure that what I had just seen was not a one-time occurrence, as well as to confirm or deny certain suspicions, I called the man with the bloody nose back as soon as I was alone in the room. It was like a fairy tale. No sooner did I call him than he was standing before me.

Are you Georg? I asked.

I thought you'd recognize me right away, Georg said, and smiled a tired, omniscient smile from the corner of his mouth, something I had never liked about him.

Where is Martha, your wife?

I was her husband; she wasn't my wife.

Why did she leave you? I asked.

She left you, not me; she was never with me. She never wanted more from me than I gave her. I existed to save her from a life in an office; I did that.

In return you kept her like a whore. Everytime you got close to her you put your hairy hand on her thigh, even on her breast, to show everyone that *this is my flesh*.

You haven't understood anything, Rosalind, she wanted to be my whore. That was her way of grasping reality. Let's not pretend it's something else, she said, this is just how people live with each other, and she too had to have a physical relationship, or else she would be afraid of going mad. If she doesn't want to sell vegetables and hasn't found some other way to be useful, it is her privilege to become a prostitute. The only way I could hurt her would have been to declare my love, which would have made her feel like a parasite. We were business partners who could give notice at any time, Martha and me. For all I cared she could have stayed; you drove her away.

Wash your face, I said quietly, I can't look at your bloody nose anymore.   Georg moistened his handkerchief with spit and wiped the blood from his nose.   Sit down, I said, she never talked about your agreement.

She thought that you knew, Georg said; later on she noticed

that you didn't have an inkling and you would have despised her had she let you in on it, despised her more than you did in the end. You despised her, didn't you?

I fell silent. Did I despise Martha? As time went by I didn't admire her anymore; the seductive power I had at first felt coming from her ceased. I remember a conversation in which I asked Martha why she didn't work and show what she could do. Although Martha had studied art history like Georg, and had graduated with decent grades, her work in a museum as a custodian was only part-time. She didn't understand my question. I do work, she said, presumably referring to her poems and drawings.

Why don't you work seriously at your profession? I asked. Martha's glance was full of estrangement. It's perverse to *think* for money, she said, it may even be against the law.

At the time I had already been working for two years in Barabas' institute, was considered a talented scholar deserving promotion; in addition to that I was obsessed by a naive ambition which drove me to challenge myself to tests of strength, to throw myself into the hardest work. I considered my will the measure of all things: throw the stone and run after it. I despised weakness, although it would never have occurred to me to say so. I would even have maintained the opposite if someone had accused me of such a thing. I would have said how deeply I was disgusted when my mother talked about people inept at living, that I even had a fatal penchant for short, delicate men. I'm certain at the time no one could have explained to me what my contempt consisted of, because I would have had to understand what I could not understand: my very lack of understanding. Since then I know that weakness can sneak up on a person the way cold invades a landscape. Suddenly and unexpectedly what was considered certain becomes unattainable; action becomes obscured by dreams; paralysis, exhaustion, beginnings are swallowed up and nothing is worth the effort anymore.

Did you despise her? Georg asked.

I don't know; I considered her weak.

Georg got up, walked slowly around the chair I was sitting in and casually placed his heavy hand on my shoulder; Georg's triumph rang in his every step. You've come a long way, haven't you, and struck my unfeeling legs, you've even managed to become a cripple, and still don't dare to think the truth. You considered Martha useless, not *useful*. Admit it, how often did you fling the word useful at her, go ahead and admit it. If she hadn't been my whore I would have considered her useless too. The only person to whom she was of measurable usefulness was me. But the funny thing is that I lost the least with her, a whore, well, you just get another one. But when I look at you, God, I think of things that puzzle me to this day; that pulled the soul right out of your body.

Not quite, not torn out, because somewhere or other the soul was still making noises, drilling paths through my flesh, out of my body, which it couldn't become one with, or it raged in this organ or that, rising in fever until I became hot and dizzy and finally put it to rest with green, red or white pills. What ought I to do with it? No longer any God to dedicate it to, no devil to sell it to. God have mercy on my soul, what to do with this sentence? What does soul mean, I said, a disagreeable product of the adrenal and the pituitary glands, the chemical state of my body, an arbitrary foggy patch of artificially excited states. There is no such thing as guilt, no such thing as sin. All that exist are predictable victims. I don't want to be a victim; I want to be guilty.

Georg continued circling me with rhythmic steps placed

like exclamation points between his words.

So you can sit lame in your chair along with your guilt and quarrel with the world. Aren't you looking for precisely my guilt in your domain?

I'll take my part, I conceded.

Georg laughed. Man fighting against his own insignificance. He prefers to heap mountains of guilt upon himself and to transform himself from an innocuous citizen into a feared villain rather than to accept mere insignificance. You lived, Rosalind, and nothing happened.

If you hadn't chased her away it would have been someone else. Martha was on the run.

I heard Georg sink onto the old sofa behind my chair; I could no longer see him. I felt uneasy.

And you, I asked, are stuck with the consequences?

Except for the children I begot, no. But that doesn't matter to me, because it doesn't matter! Regarded as a whole it is insignificant.

But your nose bleeds when you don't say the right sentences.

Ah, Rosey, I know that's the only thing that reconciled you to me: my nosebleed. Nothing more than common hypertension, high blood pressure. Don't smoke, don't get excited, and three tablets every day. I believe in medicine. My nose hasn't come up in Party files for ten years now. My nose only enhances me in your eyes; for everyone else it's a flaw, an extravagant flaw, which used to cost me five hundred marks a month, because they can't send someone to a congress with such a treacherous nose, nor to any high-level meeting; he's even useless as a supervisor for a couple of subordinates. Too high a price for the vain awareness of being a good man, don't you think, Rosalind?

I fell silent.

No, you don't think so. You've withdrawn to the certainties of evil. Do you hear the word, evil? Do you know what that is? No act or an evil act, or no act is an evil act. Why don't you answer?

What is action? I countered. What is its evil opposite? I am no longer able to say that I am doing something *because*...I can only say now, I am not doing it because I do not know why I ought to do it. And now go, get out.

*

I still consider people who are able to steal and lie as freer beings than those who can't. The ability to overstep the bounds of legality without suffering more than one gains requires either uncommon pleasure in one's own courage, and/or—this I consider even more admirable—the person no longer feels himself bound to a compelling sense of order and breaks it wherever he is able to do so without the feeling of having done something wrong. I am denied this quality due to highly pronounced moral reflexes—an ineradicable consequence of maternal upbringing. And who can tell if, equipped with a talent for lying and stealing, I might not be able, with both feet planted firmly on the ground, to master my life to its natural end? Things being as they are, however, I was left with no other possibility than to regain all the time which was no longer mine in one huge act of theft. Martha could lie and steal, which doesn't mean that she had no morals but simply that hers were of a different kind.

The first time I was with Martha when she stole I was, in spite of my hidden admiration, shocked to the point of anger. Nevertheless, it was a highly understandable, almost unavoidable theft. We wanted to buy a bottle of wine and drink it in my apartment that afternoon, when we had time for each other. The department store was overcrowded, most of the cash registers were closed and those that were open had long lines in front of them. I suggested we forget the wine. Martha stretched her narrow back, which lent her an expression of determination I had admired in her once before, reached for a shopping cart and hauled me into the crush. She took butter, bread, cheese, wine and put it all into a white plastic bag which she, as I later found out, always carried with her for such eventualities.

Martha, I whispered, Martha, stop it.

Martha laughed. Don't look like that or they'll think we're thieves, she said, and pushed me and the empty cart in front of her through the exit.

When we were once again in safety on the street, I said: You've stolen, Martha. Martha gave me a surprised look, because the sentence I had just spoken meant nothing more than she already knew. For me, however, and it proves my confusion, it meant my utmost expression of disapproval. You have stolen; was there anything worse you could say about someone? You have killed. But what more?

Martha was disappointed. Oh, Rosalind, she said, you understand less than I thought. I wanted to please you.

We were standing in the gutter, Martha carrying the bag with the stolen goods, and I felt crude and clumsy in the way I sometimes felt stiff and wooden in the presence of children.

Still, I said, not knowing what to say, I just knew that stealing was beyond my capabilities, or something like that. I just couldn't pinch, and for the first time I began to think over whether it was good or not to be able to pinch, and what prevented me from reaching for the shelf with Martha's matter-of-factness.

I just can't do it, I said.

You can learn, Martha said, I had to learn it too. When I was a child I took a boat ride with my father on a red steamship. We were attacked by pirates, but there was nothing worth stealing on the steamship. I guess the pirates had trouble finding young talent for the trade because they forced the passengers to decide to become pirates or to jump overboard, except old people and children, of course. I was already old enough. My father and I volunteered to become pirates for a year. That's where I learned everything I know. The head of the pirates was a professor of mathematics, most of the pirates were scientists, painters or poets. They came from every country you could think of and were resolved to investigate the utility of uselessness. As no one had authorized research funds for this project, they had to earn the money through piracy. One day the professor told me: two things are important, Martha. The first is, you have to find your most useless quality. For even before you were born you were included in a statistical survey in which your potential utility was calculated: the cost you incur as a child, your usability during your work phase, expected progeny, the expenses incurred in old age up until your statistically forecast age of death, in short: your profitability is estimated and is taken for granted. But you can outwit the statisticians by finding something inside yourself that they can't use. They'll install a machine in your head, they'll transform your arms into cranes, your chest into a card catalogue, your stomach into a dumping ground. But in every person there is something that they cannot use, the special, the unpredictable: soul, poetry, music, I don't know a suitable name for it, simply that thing which no one could know about before the person was born. You have to find and cherish this seemingly useless piece of you; it is the beginning of your biography.

Second, the professor said: when you have found it, you will have to learn, for good or ill, to steal in order to defend it. Whether one wants to become a thief or not, it's a simple mathematical problem in today's world. A human being lives an average of seventy years, that is twenty-five thousand five hundred fifty days, of which you have to deduct seven thousand three hundred—the first twenty years—those years in which a person is not free to do with time as he wishes; that leaves eighteen thousand two hundred fifty. You have to calculate how much of that you need for yourself and how much you can spend in pointless but profitable work, in costly techniques of survival like shopping and miscellaneous procurement activities, in decency and conventions. I'm afraid even those who are reluctant to become professional thieves are unable to manage without a little bit of theft, the professor said. We had an hour's time, which we would have wasted standing in the check-out line to buy the wine. Now we have the hour's time and the wine. There was no other way, Martha said.

Of all the peculiarities in Martha's nature, her cock and bull stories gave me the fewest problems. I met them with the same freedom in which Martha invented them. I believed her or did not believe her, as it pleased me. I derived pleasure from them in any case, and I never doubted their veracity. It was only a few years later that I gleefully began to note when Martha caught herself in contradictions and I would enumerate each inconsistent detail, playing the exultant know-it-all.

It wasn't easy to find out whether Martha's stories were true or made up, or where the border ran within the story between invention and reality. Martha had, of course, taken a trip on a steamer with her father as a child, perhaps the steamship had been red, which I doubt, however. It is also possible that there was a professor of mathematics on the steamer who taught Martha the meaning of stealing, but it is also possible that he had only given her candy, and some other person had talked about stealing or perhaps no one at all, and Martha had only made him up to lend her peculiar theories greater authority for me. That the professor was a pirate to boot was simply an extravagance which I still tolerated at the time.

The only thing I couldn't understand was why Martha so stubbornly resisted being her parents' child. The remark, which I had taken as a jest at our first meeting in the café, that Martha's mother had died as a child and that she was delivered by another woman, turned out to be something which Martha took unbelievably seriously. Her father too—I met him, a lower-echelon employee of the Berlin police— was not the man Martha talked about when she meant her father. It was really hard to imagine where these ordinary people had got the forty-eight chromosomes they had needed for Martha.

Both of them were blond and fair-skinned; I can't remember their faces, but I do know that they did not strike me as unusually beautiful or ugly. Both of them spoke Saxon dialect; they came from the area around Leipzig. Martha spoke, whenever she bothered to do so, Berlin dialect, but usually standard German. You see, Martha came to Berlin when she was still a child and was able to adjust, her mother said. Her mother was hurt more deeply than her father by Martha's statement that this man and woman were to be thanked for nourishment, clothing and a certain amount of loving care, but under no circumstances for her life. The father considered his daughter quite simply off her rocker, whereas the mother carried on a desperate struggle to be recognized as her biological parent. We had such nice pictures of her, she told me, my husband started taking photos when she was small, at Carnival in kindergarten, when she started school and when she became a Youth Pioneer. And the initiation ceremony, she had such a pretty dress, with a Stuart collar and white cuffs, pretty as a picture, but she burned all the photos, didn't leave us a one. And yet she was always well off, we never beat her, my husband didn't, and, of course, neither did I, she didn't get a single slap from us. I don't understand the girl, her mother said, and she cried. When Martha came out of the kitchen with the tea, she wiped the tears from her eyes and smiled as if she wanted to excuse herself for having lost control of her feelings again. Martha didn't notice anything of the misfortune of this woman she didn't allow to be her mother, or she pretended not to.

Martha, Rosalind whispered, Martha Mantel. Why did only she think of the things that were different between Martha and her mother? At the time she had felt a deep solidarity, deeper than she had ever felt with any human being after that, even more than with Bruno. Wasn't she now, in searching for Martha, looking for the reasons of her later betrayal? Was this the reason that her image of Martha didn't really come to life again, remaining blurred, like the silhouette in a children's coloring book, enlivened with only a few clumsily-drawn bright spots of paint?

Dawn had broken. From the stairwell and the street, sounds penetrated the building walls: rapid steps on their way to school or to the office; those who have to go to the factory

left one or two hours before. The morning odor of soap, eau
de cologne and toothpaste, concealed by cigarette smoke,
hung now in the landing. The sun used a bobbing, swaying
branch in front of the window to create wild shapes against
the white wall. Rosalind tried to bring the shadow to life.
Long black hair, a narrow back with a jutting backbone, the
soft, swinging motion of her arms. The leaves on the branch
fluttered in her shadow like captive birds, and it took a long
while before—at first indistinctly, then with increasing
clarity—a figure set itself free from the confused interplay.
Except the figure is not, as she had hoped, Martha, but
herself, Rosalind, sitting in front of a white wall, the wall
of a prison. The room in which I find myself is painted a
harsh white, the few pieces of furniture, a narrow bed, a table,
a chair, are also white. Everything is very clean. But it is
still a prison, I know. The windows are barred, the door
locked from the outside. I don't know exactly how long I've
been here, but longer than a few hours. I must have spent
the night here because the bed is rumpled and a nightgown,
with a black mark on the hem, is hanging over the chair.
I try to decipher the writing on the mark, but frequent washing
has made it illegible. I sit on the bed, uncombed and
unwashed, uneasy in these bewildering surroundings, and
I wonder whether I'm afraid. My pulse is calm, I can't feel
my stomach, my skin is cool and dry. I'm not afraid; I'm
not even excited. I'm surprised because for the longest time
there was no idea, except beatings, which made me so afraid
as being in prison. It would have to end in death, I thought,
because I would kill myself out of fear or because I would
run amok with rage and helplessness until they beat me to
a pulp. Out of fear of prison I have spent a lifetime obeying
the laws except for this one time, the one I'm here for. That

I let myself be carried away in this case surprises me as does the fact that I feel no sign of fear now. I did not act out of ignorance or impulse, although I'm sure they would like to construe it that way. It would make the case easier for everyone: a citizen with no previous police record went off the deep end. But I won't let that happen, I won't let them take my crime away from me. At the thought of the crime I feel an excitement to the point of laughter, but somehow or other it is out of the question in this bare white cell. It seems inappropriate, in light of the tangible consequences, to laugh about my crime. But when they ask me about the reason for my conduct—surely someone will come soon to call me to an interrogation—I will not try to mitigate my guilt. I will explain everything to them, even the pleasure I felt during the three hours, even when our defeat was definite—there had been no doubt of that from the first—and the last big showroom window pane shattered with a crash. I would like to know who else they've brought here among those who took part, certainly not all of them, that would be too many, only the leaders who will later be called instigators in the dossiers. Perhaps they at least let Martha go free because she is so delicate and you wouldn't think her capable of being an instigator once you see and talk to her. I saw them take Clairchen away. That took five policemen, whom Clairchen threw her two hundredweight against, by turns, so they staggered, until they finally got hold of her, on her arms, legs, head, and Clairchen could only scream filthy abuse at them. It is possible that Clairchen is sitting very close to me right now, perhaps even in the next cell, and I regret not knowing any knock signals. I remember a group of young people whom I used to laugh about because, law-abiding and free like myself, they spent their spare time in a sort of prison training. Their program included hunger exercises, sleeping and catnap exercises, and Morse code.

Suddenly the door to my cell flies open. A hunlike female steps silently into the room and casts a disapproving look at my untidy bed. Something about her person is both frightening and ludicrous, her appearance a contradiction which I feel but cannot define.

Prisoner-on-remand Polkowski, follow me, says the woman, whom I suspect is my guard. She has a deep, almost masculine voice, and I immediately understand what is fearful and ridiculous about this woman. She looks as though she had been put together from two people, as if the head of a young, slender-limbed woman had been planted atop the body of an athletic man. She is obviously aware of the paradox of her body, for she tries to adjust the expression of her soft, rosy face to the brutal effect of her body by directing her eyes stiffly at each object of her attention, constantly chomping her teeth so that her chin and jaw muscles stand out boldly under her silky skin. She locks the door of my cell. Right, she says, and I follow her. Rosalind watches in disbelief as she walks next to the guard along the white corridor. The floors are covered with a thick layer of foam rubber that absorbs every sound, and now I understand why I never heard steps from within my cell, not even before the guard opened my door. In light of her revelation, Rosalind is unable to control herself any longer. It's unbelievable, she screamed against the white wall, it's fantastic, even more fantastic than I thought. Not only can I call them all to me, I can go everywhere too, go away, open the door and leave the room. Meanwhile, undaunted by Rosalind's jubilation, I walk past the doors closely packed one after the next, without numbers or any other markings, which irritates me because this is a prison and what else is it supposed to be, and there are prison cells behind these doors and it is normal for them to have numbers. At least that's how it is in all the films I've seen about prisons. Only then do I notice that my guard is wearing a uniform I've never seen before. It's brownish violet in color and, so it seems, of good material: a light, thin wool cloth you can't buy in the stores. And there are no rank insignias. We stop in front of one of the many doors; the guard looks me over from head to foot. She is probably checking to see whether she can hand me over in this condition. Then she opens the door without knocking. Prisoner-on-remand Polkowski, she says, and disappears.

The man is standing in front of the window with his back toward me. You can sit down, he says. He is of medium height and slim, his voice sounds rather mild although—I think I can deduce this from the short sentence—he has sharpness in reserve.

You know why you are here, the man says, still with his back to me. And please do sit down.

I sit down.

Who is responsible for planning the raid? the man asks.

It wasn't a raid, and there was no plan, I say. Those arrested include Martha Mantel and Clara Winkelmann, both close friends of yours. Do you wish to maintain that all three of you just happened to be present in the department store at the same time?

Martha Mantel has been living abroad for years, and Clara Winkelmann is dead, I say; I know as I say it that I am wrong and am confused.

Please cut the funny business, the man says.

We were together, we ran out of wine, I say, relieved because I now remember exactly what happened.

Why did more than one of you go to buy wine?

I look at the back in front of the window. The man is standing very upright, does not move even when he speaks. Why doesn't he finally turn around? That's just the way it turned out, I say.

You appear not to understand the seriousness of your situation. You sabotaged provisions for the population, resisted public authority, you destroyed national property in a rowdy manner and slandered the socialist state.

That's not right about sabotage and slander, I say. When we arrived the sabotage had already begun: ten of thirteen check-out counters were closed. Nor did we slander anyone. What we said is true.

I see, the man says and turns around. He looks like Robert Redford.

Mrs Polkowski, Redford says sternly, we previously knew you to be a reasonable person; at any rate, you respected the law.

How was I known to you if I never broke the law? I say.

The man really does look like Robert Redford. Of course I know that they know everyone, but I made up my mind to tell the man everything, and that includes asking him this question which would have been superfluous in another context.

Redford smiles. If we had kept more of an eye on you, the two of us would not have to be talking right now. Perhaps we could have kept you from your indiscretion. I feel like I share part of the guilt for your misdemeanor. We should have known better what was going on inside you.

I look for a sign of scorn or mockery in Redford's face, but he really does seem concerned. Fatherly. He is not older

41

than me, how does he manage to scrutinize me in such a fatherly way?

You see, he says, in another case which we are proud of, we were able to keep a young man from doing something foolish. We observed his growing aggression, we also knew of the dangerous people he was associating with. We could see that he would soon commit a punishable offense. Shortly before that could happen we brought him in, treated his psychological deviation until he was once again a useful member of society. That took about a year, while his crime would have cost him a longer prison term. Today the boy is grateful.

I remain silent, am irritated by the man's resemblance to Redford. He offers me a cigarette. As he lights it he bends down toward me. I'm embarrassed because I'm uncombed and unwashed. I can't stand Robert Redford. All the same I cannot bear the thought that the man could find me ugly or even repulsive. As if it made any difference whether a hangman admired the neck of his victim or not. I am ashamed because I want to please the man, and I think he knows it.

Mrs Polkowski, please describe the crime in detail.

In my cell I knew exactly how I would answer this question. And now none of the sentences I have thought up are sufficient to make the man understand me.

In that case I will read you our report, he said, takes a typed sheet from his desk and reads: On Wednesday, September 17, shortly before 5:00 pm, the accused, Rosalind Polkowski, Clara Winkelmann and Martha Mantel entered the Central Provisions Facility on Becherstrasse, Pankow District, which as a result of the rush-hour shopping period just begun, was understandably frequented by more citizens than during non rush-hour periods. The three accused were inebriated. At the check-out counter they incited citizens to disregard the necessary waiting time and to take their goods through the check-out without paying. In so doing they further exploited the cries of children, which created nervousness among the citizen shoppers, in order to translate their criminal intent into action. They successfully suborned several citizens to steal national property. When the comrades of the riot police, informed by the management of the Provisions Facility, attempted to carry out their duty to restore order, the aforementioned persons barricaded the entrances in such a manner that our comrades were forced to gain entry to the premises through the display windows. The accused further scattered peas and spilled large quantities of dishwashing liquid in the aisles of the Provisions Facility, after which they dug themselves in behind the meat counter from which they threw smoked spare ribs, allocated for provisioning the populace, at members of the police force. Numerous comrades suffered injuries, including five broken legs. The crime was accompanied by repeated verbal abuse against socialist commerce and its representatives. It was not until a fire hose was brought to bear that the anti-socialist forces could be overpowered. Sum of the resulting damages: 123,456 marks.

Do you dispute the facts as depicted here? he asked.

No, I said, and tried to hide how deeply he had just hurt my feelings. He had just made my crime, which I wanted under no circumstances to have taken away from me, look ludicrous, even for me, my own crime.

Can you tell me the reasons for your misconduct?

There wasn't any other crime available at the time, I said. I didn't start the rebellion in the department store for any specific reason; I started it because I did not want to start no rebellion. The man is sitting across from me and looks me in the eyes like Robert Redford looked Katherine Ross in the eyes in *Butch Cassidy and the Sundance Kid.*

You do not have a goal, Mrs Polkowski, he says with concern in his voice. There is no meaning in your life. You know where this road leads. To loneliness, to alcoholism, to crime, to suicide. You have to find your place in society.

Although I want to stop it, although I swallow and swallow to swallow it out of existence, I hear how a laugh jumps out of my mouth into the room. It gets even worse. I start to sing. *You have a goal before your eyes.* I sing up until *for the world needs you as much as you need it.* After that I laugh again, a high-pitched, unpleasant laugh, then the attack is over, thank heaven. I find it hard to breathe.

Do you know that one, I ask the man, I sang that when I was a child. I was sure the world needed me. Since then to have a goal before my eyes I need a mirror. I am my own goal.

L'état c'est moi, Redford says, and now he laughs loudly, too loudly.

You misunderstand me, me, not the state, I say.

He becomes serious. I understand, retreat into the private sphere. But we haven't noticed that in your case, Mrs Polkowski.

I am not private, I say, I don't even know what that is. Sometimes I used to see a sign with *private path* on a small street you weren't allowed to walk on: these paths belonged to someone. I don't belong to myself. Even my secrets are secrets only because you are with us. He presses a small red button on his telephone, the door opens and my guard steps in.

That's enough, Rosalind says, the guard isn't needed now, please leave. And please sit down. The situation can change that quickly, captain or lieutenant, or whatever you were.

You are my prisoner now. It is pointless to try to escape. Relax.

The man obediently puts his right leg over his left knee.

So, Rosalind says, that was so-called role-playing. I've had you and myself believe that I incited the rebellion in the department store. An unfulfilled dream of mine. Unfulfilled, because I knew how severely you would punish such an offense. In reality I am not very brave, rather cowardly actually. Incidentally, I had imagined your methods to be different, not so mild. Has anyone ever told you how much you look like Robert Redford?

You've noticed, the man says, and proudly raises his head, which he has been propping on his hands until now. These are my work clothes, as it were. I interrogate only female inmates, my type has no effect on men. On the contrary: their reactions are more aggressive because they unconsciously take the opposing part, as do women, but their role is different. Your reaction was quite typical, almost classic: unsure, like a girl, bashful and, admit it, you wanted to please me. I am not the only artist in my department, we are employed for the most disparate age and interest groups. We have a John Lennon, an Elvis Presley, and until two or three years ago, even a Clark Gable; this comrade has since taken on Humphrey Bogart. Since we started working with these methods we have achieved quite surprising results and we can do away with the previously indispensable forms of getting at the truth, which, you can believe me, gave us no pleasure either, and have in addition, made us the constant target of the ugliest kinds of slander. The people we have to deal with should be allowed to develop trust in us. By means of public opinion polls we know whom each target group regards as the most trustworthy type of human being.

The pioneer work of the media in this area has been of inestimable value to us. They prepare the effect we desire by presenting a certain type as trustworthy over a long period of time. All we need then are good plastic surgeons and half our job is already done; the other half is achieved by the finest human feelings, such as affection, love and trust. This is always an inspiring experience.

Rosalind is growing impatient. You are beginning to gush, she said, but you have, as I can see, a meaning in your life. You have a goal before you and the world needs you.

That is correct, Redford said, and that makes me happy. Every person is happy when he feels useful. You are unhappy because you feel useless. What would be useful, Rosalind says, would it be useful to kill cats because there are too many of them, and to set a price on their pelts? We can end the conversation. Three more sentences and you'll start talking about law and order. I know that already. So long, Mister Redford, and say hello to Bogie for me.

The man dissolves silently into nothingness, and, exhausted from my encounter, I am sitting in my chair and have to think of Clairchen, who became involved unwittingly in these events, not summoned by me. I did not want to think about her anymore because every memory of Clairchen ended in the gruesome image of her death: the huge decayed body in a black dress showing against the clear blue sky. It was not found until the leaves fell from the trees and way up, at the top of a chestnut tree, the corpse and the limb where Clairchen had hanged herself became visible. No doubt they would have noticed the stench sooner if she hadn't lived near a slaughter house, which already smelled of rotten meat. One reads in the Notebooks of Malte Laurids Brigge: *Who places*

any value these days on a well finished death…, the desire
to have a death of one's own is becoming rarer and rarer.
Before much longer it will become as rare as a life of one's
own.

Clairchen had both, a life of her own and a death of her
own, and no other death could have been more fitting to her
extravagant life than this shocking, disgusting and brutal sign
of helplessness. In her plump body Clairchen harbored an
immoderate longing for love whose natural impossibility of
being fulfilled drove her to desperate excesses. She was said
to have raped both men and women. Every offense, inten-
tional or unintentional, that she suffered, was punished by
robbing the offender. She took whatever was at hand: a gold
ring or a handful of change out of a jacket pocket. I was missing something after almost every visit by Clairchen although
I didn't have the vaguest idea of how I might have offended
her. I sometimes found the missing objects, carelessly thrown
in the corner of a shelf, in her apartment. Then I got them
back. In order to hurt Clairchen it was sufficient not to love
her. In order to be loved she got caught in webs of lies, gave
away what she owned and didn't own—borrowed books,
stolen money—she flattered, slandered and even painted her
bizarre paintings in order to be loved. As soon as she succeeded in coaxing feelings of love from a person, whether
a man or a woman, she pounced with the same stubborn woo-
ing on someone else, in order to suck a drop of love out of
him as well, as a mosquito sucks blood from a human body.
Clairchen's lust for love was insatiable, and Martha said that
no one could help Clairchen, because she herself did not consider herself lovable and therefore needed daily, hourly proof
to the contrary.

One day Clairchen revealed to us that she was expecting

a child. Martha was horrified. She told Clairchen the address of a doctor in Dimitroffstrasse. All we have to do is get a VIP to register you there; he only performs abortions for VIPs, Martha said. Clairchen shook her head.

Clara, Martha said, you had a dancing mouse, goldfish and a striped parakeet. None of them lasted more than two weeks in your place because you forgot to feed them.

A kid's no parakeet, Clairchen said, besides, I didn't forget, I just couldn't hack it.

I fell silent. From the time I found out that I couldn't have children I had the same dream again and again: I gave birth to a child through my ear; the baby crawled, painlessly and warm, through my left ear like the daughter of Indra did through her father's ear. I didn't consider whether I really wanted a child, but I did not feel qualified to advise others in this sort of matter. I also thought it possible that a child could free Clairchen of her fear of not being loved.

As long as the child—visible only as Clairchen's immensely arched abdomen—was growing inside its mother, Clairchen enjoyed the care and attention that she and the child were given. This was also the first time that her shapeless body acquired a certain legitimacy, and the clear signs of pregnancy placed her beyond all scorn. The baby was a girl, Clairchen named it Carmen, and we asked ourselves whether this name concealed a hope or the first rejection to come, for a few weeks before that Clairchen had said: If it's a girl that means there'll be two monsters, but if it's a mutant she'll be real pretty and understand me as little as the rest of ya.

Clairchen tried hard: she read books about infant care, carried the baby around with her like a kangaroo with its pouch; she even breastfed her. We thought for three months that she had calmed down and that the baby could really have

48

offered her the huge amount of love she needed to live. Then she took it to her mother in Brandenburg, where she visited it now and again. Mom's got a garden, she said.

She can't help it, Martha said, none of us can help it because we learn it the wrong way. Love was one of the main areas of research for the pirates, who carried out exhaustive studies in which they had found that throughout the entire area of European culture there was a close relationship between love and submission in its active and passive forms. The European infant becomes acquainted with love as an act of submission; the first being it loves is simultaneously the embodiment of power: the mother. She can prohibit, punish, is even allowed to strike, she can let the baby starve to death or succor it. The more clearly the European infant proves its submission and obedience, the more certain it can be of her love. The mother's love is the reward for obedience, and submission is the condition for her love, upon which, once again, the baby's life depends. As a result, the feelings of Europeans in love are an inextricable chaos of affection, lust for power, masochistic servility, and it would be natural to assume that people who love each other in this way often use extortionary methods with one another. This, at any rate, is what she said the professor had told her back then. There are only differences of degree between Clairchen's behavior and ours: we are less afraid, Martha said.

Clairchen lived for another five years after her child was born. I had already received Martha's postcard by the time she died: Am in Spain, looking for my father. Martha. I didn't go to Clairchen's burial, especially since we hadn't seen each other since Martha's disappearance.

I did not want to think about Clairchen, and now that I was forced to do so I will forego elaborating my possible guilt in her demise. That would be hypocritical. I'm not interested in guilt anymore—mine or others—and when I said before that I wanted to be guilty, I really meant that I wished to be the cause of an effect. Seen in this way there is no connection between myself and Clairchen's death, and even if I were out to find myself guilty at any price, I could not do so. Although the details of my life are, of course, more familiar to me than those of others, much of its real meaning is hidden from me, and at various times I find very different explanations for why it has turned out as it has. But for me Ida's and Clairchen's lives have clear, at times even unequivocal meaning. This is, I fear, nothing more than an illusion based on my ignorance of their secrets: the hundred thousand concealed coincidences or their own inscrutability. In addition one knows the life of others—insofar as one doesn't take part in it directly—primarily through stories, that is, it has already been structured into its seemingly causal pattern, whereas one's own life, which is only experience, appears like a puzzling mass of knots and snares, and it is left to each mood or simply to chance to determine the flux of detail.

I find it very easy to understand a story like that of Hans and Ida. Hans was a worker at the Royal Porcelain Factory, and Ida was learning the trade from master tailor Kramer, who had taken her on for the sake of Ida's family. Ida had been sickly and nervous since birth, and my mother said that when she was young her sister had suffered from a kind of St Vitus Dance. Hans and Ida got to know each other one afternoon when Ida was eating pea soup and bockwurst at Aschinger's. Hans liked Ida's red hair and white skin. He started a conversation and treated her to a cup of coffee, a very common form of becoming acquainted at the time, as

Ida later declared to me on numerous occasions. Ida fell in love with him, and he with Ida. A year later they became engaged and opened a joint savings account. These were the six happiest years of my life, Ida said, and the photographs of her from that time seem to prove it.

Ida and Hans are standing at an angle open to the viewer, half next to, half across from each other, with only the outer surfaces of their hands—Ida's left and Hans' right—touching. Ida is wearing a satin dress; Hans a dark suit with light leggings. Clearly they were posing for the photographer, although behind the pose is a smile each has for the other, whose meaning the viewer can only guess. The six happiest years in Ida's life ended with a phone call in which Hans told his fiancée that the situation had become too difficult for him, an Aryan engaged to a Polish half-Jew, and that Ida, who loved him after all, would understand. He sent her half of the money they had saved, by mail. Ida lost ten pounds that week and had a fit of St Vitus Dance.

For an outsider this is an obvious case: Hans was a weak man who could not bear up under the circumstances. But what if Hans had begun to love another woman in the meantime or had stopped loving Ida; what if he believed that under the difficult circumstances, which neither of them could influence, he would hurt her less this way than by admitting his feelings for her were spent. And what if this never-ending male-female struggle had long existed between Hans and Ida, but had merged into a larger cruel struggle and had later been forgotten by Ida? Would the story of Ida and Hans still have been clear-cut or would it have become one of the many enigmatic love affairs left unhealed by history, whose logical meaning Ida could never fathom? She would have known no more about it than I did about Bruno and me. Like myself, she would have had to search for the beginnings of her failure in the confusion of words and gestures, to set off her own failure against that of the partner in order to find something that made sense; something to complete the sentence: it happened that way because.... But as things were, Ida's small love belonged to the period, as a tiny cell does to the organism which caused it to grow, and the finitude of this love acquired meaning through the barbarity of a time that a gentle and weak man like Hans was not up to.

And we, Bruno, Rosalind said, what do we have to explain our end: a too small apartment, an unloving father, alcohol, the government, boredom, soccer, Barabas, the atom bomb, the kitchen sink, you think that's enough, I knew I'd find you here, put the beer down Bruno, it's at least your tenth, I can see it in your eyes.

Bruno turned around slowly and leaned his back against the counter. He kept the beer glass in his hand. Rosa, Bruno said, Rosa Polkowski, the lady with the Burgundian pride, descended into the cesspool of alcoholism. *Salve Regina.* He kissed Rosalind's hand. As always when Bruno was drunk he spoke slowly, drawing out his vowels voluptuously as though he were singing them, while he accompanied his words with the gesticulations of an opera singer. Twenty beers, thirty beers, forty beers, Bruno said, the world has never seen a happy man except for the drunk. Schopenhauer. Did you come to interrupt my happiness?

You're drunk, Rosalind said.

What a sentence, Bruno said, what a sentence, he repeated loudly and stretched his arms out in front of him with a broad gesture. Am I drunk? Of course I'm drunk. Who has the nerve not to be drunk? Who's the greedy arsekissing knave who doesn't want to be drunk?

The men who were standing nearby, three of whom Rosalind recognized, laughed in agreement, which induced Bruno to continue his speech. He lowered his voice, turned his head to one side and gently placed his hand on Rosalind's shoulder, such that his whole posture expressed indulgence. Did you come to tell me that you're sober now, he said, and do you mean to say that you're a better person for it? No, you don't think that, Rosa, you're not that far gone.

I want to know why you went off back then, Rosalind said.

Because you'd have beaten me to death if I hadn't. Bruno flourished his beer glass in the air and called past Rosalind's head: Well then, cheers! You'd have beaten me to death, and you really oughtn't to beat me to death, Rosa. They'd have thrown you in jail and me they'd have thrown, eternally sober, into a grave or as dry powder into an urn.

Well, well, well, said an elderly gentleman with a dark blue-silver polka dot tie, who suddenly popped up behind Bruno. Rosalind recognized him as the sinologist named Baron, known as the Count by the bar regulars. Bruno had raised him to this title ten years ago after the scholar, highly regarded by experts in the field of European sinology, had received the Pin of Honor for German-Soviet Friendship, GESOV for short, for his work as treasurer of that association. But that wouldn't be in keeping with your standards, the Count said, shuddered, to show his disgust at such a fate and disappeared again behind Bruno's back, as if frightened of his own meddling.

Why, Rosa, do you say that I left you, since I didn't leave you; and why did you leave me, Rosa? Bruno asked, falling gracefully into the posture of someone looking at a painting, by stepping back a step with his right leg, while he left the other foot where it was, pointed slightly outward, without turning his searching glance from Rosalind's face.

Pardon me, Brünoh, the Count said over Bruno's shoulder, but we have a tautology here, just so this won't pass by unnoticed; a tautology: dry powder! Moist powder would be mud, thick mud, slush, mush. Just to make sure it doesn't pass by unnoticed. The Count sniggered or coughed slightly, guiltily, and quickly disappeared again. He always pronounced Bruno's name the French way because its German version sounded vulgar, *ergo* unsuitable for Bruno.

You left *me*, Rosalind said through the jumble of deep male voices, beer fumes and cigarette smoke. Why?

Bruno sighed. Most misfortune arises from the fact that people can't keep things to themselves, there's simply nothing they can keep to themselves, they can't even keep the ineffable to themselves. Bruno sat down at an empty table and looked sadly into his almost empty beer glass. No one asks: why are you staying, Bruno said, everyone asks why are you going, but you only need reasons for staying; leaving is natural. Anyone who stays has won a struggle against his nature. We lost the battle against ourselves, Rosa.

Rosalind kept silent. It now occurred to her that it would have been impossible earlier on to talk about their life together. Rather than become involved in a discussion about the housekeeping or something of the sort, Bruno would change his habits, seemingly without effort, in the way Rosalind wanted him to, without her ever asking him to do so. A lack of adaptability is the sign of disturbed self-confidence, Bruno said. The waiter replaced Bruno's empty glass with a full one, half of which Bruno drank in a single draught, washing down with it the melancholy of the last few minutes. He slowly got up, keeping his balance with difficulty, and when he stood up he said so loud that the other tipplers could hear him once more: You just couldn't forgive me for knowing Latin. Everyone laughed, Bruno along with them; not a nasty laugh, not even derisive or malicious, simply the cheerful, unanimous laughter of those who have won. Nor could one assume that the laughers—except for the Count—also knew Latin, but Bruno was one of them, which meant that his special ability became collective property, embellishing everyone who felt part of the group. Suddenly Bruno grew serious, cast a tired glance into the group, made a throw-away gesture and said: The rabble laughs, the rabble laughs... Now the Count chuckled secretively while anger grew in the eyes of some of those who had just applauded Bruno.

The fact that Bruno had a number of abilities Rosalind did not—Latin, playing the piano, driving a car, chess, lifting heavy objects, French, the list was longer—had burdened their relationship. It was only in the first months that Rosalind had felt undivided admiration for Bruno's allround talents, which she soon felt to be equally threatening. There was no field, not even her own, history, in which she felt safe from Bruno's superior knowledge, which she often called a know-it-all attitude, quite aware that she was being unfair to him. Being almost the same age, she wondered where Bruno could have gathered all his knowledge; and the answer—that Bruno had already read all the most important books, taught himself music and art by age twenty-two—completely disheartened her, and put her at odds with her heredity and sex. Bruno's father—until his death, head physician in a large clinic— came from a family with a long medical tradition; his mother, a baroness, spent her youth between her parents' estate in Pomerania and her studies in Paris. Although the parents were not especially involved in the education of their sons Bruno and Robert—except for additional Latin lessons—they did offer them an intellectual environment that was unusual in the country between the rivers Elbe and Oder, and which, moreover, was vilified as bourgeois.

Rosalind's parents—her father was a machinist, her mother a telephone operator; both became teachers in a crash program after the war and her father's return from POW camp—had obtained that little bit of knowledge necessary for their new profession with great effort, and had broadened it during the following years at Party schools and similar institutions where they learned the science of the new world view according to the changing catechisms of the times.

These differences of background were regrettable, they were, however, beyond Rosalind's criticism or self-criticism. They were inalterably given. It was a different matter with the omissions brought on by herself, most of which Rosalind blamed less on her abilities than on her gender. During the years in which Bruno had apparently read everything that could add to his general knowledge, from Homer through Lawrence Sterne and Hölderlin up to Kafka, Rosalind had spent her time stumbling from one love affair to the next. All of them were more or less unhappy and enervating, and her system of garnering knowlege was the result of the peculiarities of each lover. Rosalind's interests were thus variously medicine, theater, classical languages, photography, philosophy, even mathematics for a short while. She studied beginner's Polish, Spanish and Hungarian, and while she was still working on her degree, she attended a drawing course for a few weeks because she had fallen in love with an art student. Although she always found this sort of behavior ridiculous, swearing after each affair not to let herself be carried away in the future by similar attacks of unchecked and melodramatic feelings, she was unable to stop repeating them, thereby increasing her heartache over unrequited or insufficient love through the agony of self-contempt. She considered her inability to subordinate her behavior to her own judgment a shameful defect in her character until she noticed that this type of conduct, common among women, almost never happened to men. She really did not envy Bruno his knowledge, but as soon as she realized that she would never catch up to him, she was filled with rage against her own inadequacy, against the injustice of nature which had equipped her with hormones causing so many different effects, rage against the endless talk of young and beautiful femininity, which she was part of whether she liked it or not. In the final analysis it was directed against herself as well, on the one hand because she thought she was not up to these demands, on the other because she was not indifferent to them.

Bruno mumbled softly to himself, beating a soft rhythm to his words with the fingertips of this right hand; Rosalind could make out...*in the deep slumber of the Hermaphrodite...*

I've long since forgiven you for your Latin, she said to Bruno, I don't need it any longer 'cause now I know Eskimo.

What do you know?

Eskimo.

Bruno laughed so hard tears came to his eyes.

Are you crying? Rosalind asked.

I'm so touched, Bruno said, Count, please come here, Rosa can speak Eskimo.

Shall I say a sentence, Rosalind said, I'll say a sentence in Eskimo, okay?

Three, the Count said, at least three, you can't check someone's knowledge of a language with only one sentence.

While Rosalind was thinking over which three sentences

to use to prove she knew Eskimo, the Count said: Rosa, I envy you, truly envy you, for having a language in which one has yet to think one's thoughts. I must know about twenty languages, isn't that right, Brünoh? One doesn't count them, and I've thought my way through all of them, but I haven't added much new to them over the years. Quite the contrary, only the painful memories of the ecstasies of past newness: the first conversation in Greek, the first dream in Chinese, the first poem in Japanese.

The mention of his first Japanese poem brought a wistful smile to the Count in memory of his bride Tsugiko from Kyoto. Ten years ago the Count was permitted to live in Kyoto for six months, under the auspices of a national academic exchange program, to study the famous collections of Japanese art there. It was only thanks to fair Tsugiko, the Count later told, that he did not succumb to a mysterious disease, the so-called Kyoto Disease, which many scholars from all over the world have fallen victim to. Its cause is puzzling. The climate plays a role, but most of all the rare chances of visiting exhibitions and museums. Some of them were open only once or twice in six months in order to pro-tect their treasures from variations in temperature and exposure to light, which meant that everyone who was sick or impeded on this one day had to wait five or six months to be able to make up what he or she had missed. So it was that foreigners soon lost all sense of time and, favored by the beauty of the city, quickly fell into a blissful lethargy in which they soon forgot the purpose of their stay, often not beginning their journey home for ten or twenty years…some never returned. When the Count met Tsugiko he was already suffering the first symptoms of the Kyoto Disease—drowsiness and forgetfulness—without noticing it himself, and it was only love that brought his senses back to life. Six months later he left Tsugiko behind as his bride. Since then they have written each other regularly. Tsugiko wrote in Japanese, the Count wrote in German for reasons of linguistic pedagogy, although he included notes in Japanese in his letters on etymological and grammatical forms, to help Tsugiko translate them. Once Tsugiko visited the Count in Berlin, but had to return to Kyoto after four weeks because her parents urgently needed her help in their small dyehouse. The Count received his last letter from Japan two and a half years ago; still, he talked about his bride and about the piano he had bought her five years ago, which he kept in his basement covered with blankets.

A new language is like a new life, the Count said, isn't it, Brünoh? and Bruno agreed.

I'll now say the first sentence, Rosalind said: Tuluvkap orssok tingupa. Now the second: ernerpit titorfinguak tiguva. And the third: Aningaussat upernak ilingnut nagsiussaka tiguvigit. Did you hear, three sentences.

And the Count said: Zaì xiuzhèngzhugì luxiàn kòngzhì de dìfāg, huáiren bù choù, hǎvrén bù xiáng.

And Bruno said: Arma virumque cano, Troiae qui primus ab oris Italiam fato profugus laviniaque venit litora.

And Rosalind said: Inokatiminik mamardlîssartok ugperissagssáungilax.

And the Count: Zhǎn chū de měishù zuò pǐn, weí dàguān.

And Bruno: Multum ille et terris iactatus et alto vi superum...

And Rosalind: Niune napivâ erdluvdlune.

They talked this way for a while, each in his own language, and the laughter with which they accompanied their talk came from both the common fact of each having a language of his own, and from the fun of thus being able to tell the others the most gruesome secrets while simultaneously keeping them to themselves. The fact that none of them actually spoke a real secret did not diminish the enjoyment in the possibility of doing so.

Of course the Count could have understood Bruno, but he was so completely absorbed in Chinese that it was not hard for him to forget his knowledge of Latin for the moment. Initially, a number of the guests had followed the three, but had later moved back out of boredom or mistrust when it became apparent that they did not want the others to take part.

A round for the three of us, Bruno called.

And the Count, who couldn't resist the temptation, used the interruption to ask whether they ought not to attempt a translation. Bruno had no objection, but Rosalind said that she wasn't ready to translate anything today, it was so nice that she could say something the other two could not understand, she'd like to enjoy it a little longer.

The Count was disappointed, and Bruno comforted him, saying that it always starts like this, but that things would turn out differently in time. The Count finished his beer and got up with a brief bow to Rosalind. *Le devoir nous appelle, Madame*, he said, and when she turned to Bruno again he too was gone. As she spoke his name, Bruno, I hear myself say, I sit back in my chair, alone, and would like to curse out loud in Eskimo, but I've forgotten how.

I don't want to end the scene like this. I want Bruno to tell me why he left me although I know the reason; but what does Bruno know. His claim that he had not left me, but I him, is absurd. Bruno packed his bag before my eyes—except for his books everything he owned fit into a medium-sized travel bag—he had packed his bag, put his key on the table and then slammed the door shut behind him, not loudly but clearly, a laconic scene as in a film: ridiculous and unforgettable. I close my eyes in order to concentrate and try to summon Bruno here, into my apartment, am, however, interrupted after a few seconds by the shuffling, hissing and crackling from the furthest corner of the room. The man in the red uniform, the woman with a mind of her own, the man with the bloody nose, the woman with the high voice, the man with the unhappy childhood and the woman with the gentle nature are sitting silently around the table, and I am mad because I have such imperfect control over my miraculous ability, thereby once again enabling unauthorized persons to interfere with my inquiries. The intruders seem neither to notice nor miss me; instead they talk without the slightest embarrassment.

Second Interlude

The man in the red uniform:
> Quiet, ladies and gentlemen, do not get the idea that this is a cozy chat. The topic is earnest, the time is earnest. We are talking about the smallest blister, as Marxengels said, the smallest amniotic sac of society, and if it bursts the family is dead. This is why the core hearth of humanity has to keep boiling. Understood?

The woman with a mind of her own:
> Yes, indeed, lock 'em up, lock 'em up: adulterers, queers, unwed mothers. But you pamper them and they multiply. People like us have to work ourselves to the bone and pay taxes.

The man with the unhappy childhood:

Oh, God, I'm with these people again, but I'm not going
to arrest anyone this time, I'm not going to let myself
be seduced by you again.

The woman with a mind of her own:

Here we have it, all over again, seduced, it always starts
with seduction. Shut your mouth, you sick mother-killer.

The man in the red uniform:

Enough of your private matters, there are no private matters here. I have the floor. Who would like to make a
scholarly statement on the problem of the smallest
amniotic sac?

The woman with the high voice raises her hand and is given
the floor by the man in the red uniform:

How splendid it was back then when Papa used to come
home at night and we used to read the letter from
Mommy and Aunt Friedi together. Papa called me
Mommy and called Papa Papa, and our children called
us Mommy and Papa. We lived on the sunny side of
our street and were a happy family. And now...

The woman with the high voice starts to cry, and is unable
to continue speaking.

The man with the bloody nose:

If we have to talk about marriage you might as well call
a doctor immediately. I despise married couples. I always
recognize them, I'd recognize their smell even with my
eyes closed. As soon as a married couple appears
together, the one part takes on the odor of the other:
the man smells of the woman, the woman smells of the
man, together they exude a breath-taking composite odor
of aftershave, lipstick, toilet soap and feminine hygiene
spray. A four-legged, chemically scented neuter.

The woman with the gentle nature interrupts:

Oh, no, this is mediocre. I hate mediocrity. I would much rather Piti worked in a factory than be a mediocre musician. When he's mediocre I can't love him. I can only love the outstanding. Piti knows that. Piti said to me just yesterday: Tipi, you are quite outstanding because you love outstanding things so much. And Piti also had a quite outstanding warmth when he told me that. Right after that I wrote a pretty poem about it, and our daughter Antigone said: my mommy can do everything: write poems, sing, paint, knit, cook. Oh: that's my goal: to be outstanding. And Piti too tries hard not to disappoint me. Sometimes he doesn't manage it and is mediocre again. Piti, I tell him, Piti, if you become mediocre I'll have to divorce you.

The man in the red uniform:

Destructive, it's all destructive. I forbid you to think destructively. I would ask you please for a constructive, scholarly contribution.

The woman with a mind of her own:

My own mind is very constructive. Why do we have progress? Leave it to the computers to decide who gets whom. Marriage at twenty-one, divorce outlawed and that's that. I've been married now for thirty years and am still alive. The man is still alive, too.

The man with the bloody nose:

Don't forget the murder statistics in your deliberations. A high murder rate makes no better an impression than a high divorce rate.

The woman with the high voice:

Oh, how terrible, if Papi had killed me.

The man with the unhappy childhood:

What did you do to make him want to kill you? Did you

say he couldn't play with toy trams, did he always have to eat when the food was on the table, did you alwaysforce him to use the second towel from the right and the left half of your marriage bed; you yelled at him when he didn't come home on time or bought meat with too much fat. Oh, then you have reason to be afraid. They have forbidden me to get a divorce, she and my mother, and how often have I hoped something would happen to her so she would have to go to the hospital at least for a little while.

The man in the red uniform:

Law and discipline! Discipline and law! As you are incapable of scholarly thought I am putting an end to the seminar and am going to give a report. Pencil, paper, take notes. First: the man without a family. The man without a family bears no responsibility, we call that irresponsible, and as such represents a threat to law and order. His present whereabouts are often unknown, which means that there is even doubt as to whether he can receive his induction notice in time. He thinks that he is only able to make decisions for himself and is prone to quit his job spontaneously and change apartments. In addition, he spends his money haphazardly, buys goods outside the regular inventory, thereby breaking the continuous supply of the full assortment of goods. Summary, write this down: the man without family spends two-thirds of his time unsupervised and is therefore to be classified as a risk.

The woman with the high voice:

That's what I told Papi: think about the family. One time Papi wanted to lodge a complaint about his boss; I told him, you can't do that and think about your family. Then

Papi thought about the family and saw very quickly that he couldn't lodge a complaint. You are not allowed to be self-centered in a family.

The woman with the gentle nature:

Would you cut that out with your Papi. Do you know how mediocre that sounds? I think you are very mediocre. Your hairdo, your dress, everything about you is mediocre. And you make an unpleasant impression when you cry all the time. If you were pleasant you would still have your husband and wouldn't have to cry.

The man with the bloody nose presses the handkerchief against his nose:

This time it comes from laughing, he says. I was just thinking of two ladies I know and their speeches about the oppression of women. A man's relationship to marriage is one of decay. The more decayed he is, the easier he finds it to put up with marriage. In his death-throes his final resistance is broken.

The man in the red uniform bellows:

Keep it down to a dull roar!

The others fall silent, aghast:

Well, then, take notes. Second: the woman without family. The woman without family is divided into two groups: (a) the woman without family, without child (b) the woman without family, with child. Both groups are in turn subdivided into groups (aa) and (ba): the woman who is involuntarily without family, with or without child. The woman voluntarily without child (aa) is similar to the man without family in her behavior. She is, however, to be regarded as more dangerous, as she is equipped with additional, strongly anarchistic tendencies. She is, fortunately, still a rare phenomenon. The woman voluntarily without family with child (ba) resembles (aa) yet complements the above behavior through a clever tactic of refusal. Under the guise of maternal responsibility she backs out of important social activities such as standing in honor guards, demonstrating and attending meetings. Now on to the greatest danger: the woman involuntarily without family with and without children (bb and ab). They form a potential for feministic subversion through their permanent discontent. They attack men, propagate love between women and thus, see Marxengels, burst the smallest amniotic sac. Steps, write this down: compulsory marriage by law, reintegration of released prisoners via compulsory assignment to marriage partners, no apartments to be granted to unmarried women.

The woman with a mind of her own:

As a mother I have to say, keep my son out of this; use your own children instead. Hand my son over to a female criminal?

The man with the unhappy childhood:

It is regrettable that I never learned how to laugh, otherwise I could make up my mind now whether I think this is all a laughing or a crying matter.

The woman with the gentle nature:

I really have to get hold of myself, mister, but you see, I'm smiling, aren't I, I don't give the impression of being coarse, although I am outraged because you want to prevent both progress and the outstanding.

The man in the red uniform talks in a staccato and pounds on the table with every word:

Progress takes place scientifically, that means, as Marxengels says, that the new grows within the old like a child inside its mother. We have a law protecting mothers-to-be and nursing mothers, and therefore a mother has to be taken care of, yes, more: she must be made to flourish so that it grows within her. This is historicaldialectics, is that clear?

It's clear, Rosalind said to the man in the red uniform, who, surprised at her unexpected agreement, looked up and, when he discovered Rosalind, put his right hand to the visor of his red cap and gave her a military salute. I think it's utterly unreal that I really used to know people like you, Rosalind said, but since you are present in my memory I must have run across you in my real life. I have no doubt of that. If I say that I am, in the end, truly grateful for your uninvited appearances here, you'll probably misunderstand me. I'll say it nonetheless. You can go now.

*

It seemed to Rosalind in retrospect that she had lived in two different worlds. Whatever was right in one was wrong in the other, and even such simple concepts as good and evil did not mean the same thing in each. The one language existed in the other like a secret language, although it consisted of the same words. And since she had been unable to draw a dividing line between a simple and a two-fold life either as a child or later on, she concluded that it had been the determining factor of her life from the very beginning. The most important difference between the two worlds was in how they treated mystery. In the world that included her parents, school, Ida and, later, the Barabas institute, mystery was regarded with contempt; it was considered something which, to the extent it was recognized at all, had to be eliminated immediately by being aired. A mystery had to be aired like a foul-smelling toilet or a room heavy with sweat. Something forbidden, crazy notions, lies were assumed to be behind mysteries. In this world the most everyday explanations were found for the most peculiar happenings. Does God exist? Did you ever see him, Rosi, no one has seen him, that means that he doesn't exist. I prayed to him all the same, just to be safe.

For the other world, mystery and the inexplicable meant nothing less than the ineffable connection of things and of us ourselves who move among them. The usual statement, that the connection between things and ourselves is a mystery, simply gives the impression of expressing the same thing in a more realistic way. It does not show respect for mystery and its infinite nature. In this world it's considered more important to know the mystery than to air it; one can't resist its pull, one comes as close to it as one can without disputing its existence. The first big mystery I remember was that God let shepherd's purse grow on Tempelhof Field when I asked him to. All I had to do was to climb into the round hole in the earth that someone, perhaps an anti-aircraft volunteer, had dug long ago in the meadow and which you climb down into on a small iron ladder. Down there, closely surrounded by the threatening bare earth, which at the same time made me feel at home and protected me from the looks of strangers, I had to say softly and clearly with eyes closed and hands folded: please, dear God, let more white flowers bloom for me. After that I had to wait for a moment to give God some time, and when I left my secret prayers, I would be sure to find some of those white flowers I sought more as food than to admire, because the small heart-shaped pulp in their stems was edible and tasted better than dried potatoes. I could repeat this trade with God as often as I liked, I never got so much out of it that I could have abused the preciousness of His gift, and never so little that I had to doubt God's existence and mercy.

Every occurrence can be a mystery and no mystery, depending on how you look at it, Martha said. She herself preferred to regard things as mysteries in order to find out more about them.

Take love, Martha said. Its coming and going is an utter mystery to man. An excitement comes over a person, Proust said, and the result is that the person has to fall in love with whoever happens to be sitting next to him. You see, it's like the greylag geese: they crawl out of their eggs and the first thing they see is their mother; even if it's a tin can, they have to follow it from then on. Something within us awakens, and we have to love the first thing we see until the excitement leaves us again. That is the mystery. But nowadays they come and ask why. They measure the secretion of adrenalin, compile statistics about duration, course, resistance-to-wear probability, and separation factor, and all the answers they are looking for begin with *because*. It is this way *because*...One day they will know all the chemical and physical facts of being in love and will prescribe pills for us against lover's grief. Our states of excitement will cease, anyone can sit next to us without us falling in love, and the problem will be solved. The professor said that anyone who wants to experience the fascination of a mystery has to surrender himself to it, not destroy it. Unfortunately he said, people feel so inordinately threatened in their security by every phenomenon that doesn't fit into their system of order that they immediately attack it with everything they have. This, the professor said, was the real danger. I don't know whether it's really dangerous,

Martha said, in any case it's deadly dull.

The café was half empty; the soccer world championship final was on television. Martha and Rosalind sat across from one another without looking at each other. Martha ran her index finger across the rim of her glass until it began to emit a soft singing tone.

What, Rosalind asked, is deadly dull?

Martha's finger was still circling the rim of the glass; the vibrations had begun to produce a thin, screeching sound.

I asked you something, Rosalind said.

Martha wasn't listening. She seemed to have become one with the ever more piercing sound, which vibrated with an urgent tension that grated on Rosalind. It wasn't the first time that she had felt irritated by Martha's absurd trains of thought. Rosalind's life had changed since she belonged to the Barabas institute. She had learned to allocate her thoughts for weeks or months to a single topic, to steer them in a certain direction and to bring them to a concrete result—Barabas called that purposeful, scholarly thinking. She used to get up every morning at six o'clock and seldom returned home before six in the evening, while Martha slept until she had had enough sleep, thought what she wanted to and how she wanted to, by leaps and bounds, dreamily and, as Rosalind noticed a number of times, almost childlike. It also seemed to her that Martha's reveries had lost most of their brilliance; she used to think up entire stories, whereas lately she had limited herself to aphorisms in which she repeated herself more than once. The path of virtue is lined with flowers having heart disease, was one of the favorite sayings Martha used in Rosalind's company. Rosalind most frequently accused her of being financially dependant on Georg, a state of affairs she described as the parasitic existence of a slave. Martha said she saw little difference between Barabas and Georg, at best the fact that Georg was an individual, whereas Barabas was only a single person in a whole hierarchy of superiors running all the way up to the head of state. The only thing missing in your slave's existence is the parasitic aspect, Martha said.

It would have been pointless to try to communicate to her some of the pleasure Rosalind felt when one of her research projects was a success or when her opinion won out against someone else's, when she even succeeded in forcing Barabas to give in. Martha would have retreated into incomprehension or into one of her absurd sentences. Rosalind watched Martha, the way she was sitting across from her without looking up, with all her concentration focused on her agonizing game with the glass. She was wearing a sweater that was much too loose, whose sleeves covered half her hands, leaving only her thin, childlike fingers free. The screeching of the glass crescendoed menacingly, and Martha's face was distorted into a fearful rapacity. Then there was a screech, a human scream, which shattered it at the highest pitch. The murdered glass fell onto the table in two pieces.

The wrong questions, Martha said.

Which questions? Rosalind asked.

The deadly dull wrong questions, Martha said.

Without introduction, as she began playing cautiously with the pieces, she said: Are you coming along to America?

Ship or plane? Rosalind asked.

Or to Greenland? Martha said.

Rosalind declined with a gesture. Oh, Martha.

The worst thing about it is that there are no strangers anymore, Martha said, there aren't any or I don't recognize them. Some of the people I know I can't possibly know and yet I know them. I met a girl yesterday whom I went to school with. Her name was Barbie Hollerbusch and she looked like an American Indian, but had eyes that were as blue as any I've ever seen. I never saw a woman who looked even remotely like her. Until yesterday. I met her, in person, yesterday, which is impossible because she drowned two years ago. Moreover, the woman I saw yesterday was twenty years old at most. Barbie Hollerbusch would be thirty now. I followed the girl, even asked her how to find a street. She walked like Hollerbusch, talked like her, laughed like her. I meet more and more people whom I think I went to school or kindergarten with. Most of the time they're either too old or too young, but I know them all.

Maybe we're repeating ourselves, Rosalind said, every ten years the same assortment of people is born, it might be possible, you know. Some variety or other dies out because they can't stand the air anymore, and a new, more robust one is added. Barbie Hollerbusch's type just hasn't died out yet.

That would be awful, Martha said.

What?

That would mean that I really know everyone. No strangers anymore, no mystery, only copies. She placed her hands on the edge of the table with her palms opened and looked for a way out on the lines of her palms.

So you believe every bit of alchemist bullshit now, do you? Rosalind said.

Martha closed her hands to loose fists. It doesn't matter what I believe, she said, there are no strangers anymore, I can see that.

How do you expect to meet strangers in your life, Rosalind said, you sit at home, in the café, now and then you go to your museum and make sure nobody steals the paintings, or you come to me and are disappointed that you don't find ten strangers waiting for you in the kitchen.

Do you meet strangers? Martha asked.

I'm glad if I don't have to see any. That's the difference.

My father, Martha said, told me that when he was young he met a lottery ticket vendor who sold destinies on the street. My father didn't buy any because he was afraid of getting gypped. He never forgave himself.

Two weeks later Martha vanished. No one knew how or where until the postcard arrived from Spain. Am in Spain, looking for my father. Martha. She must have already known that evening in the café that she would leave; she leave, I stay.

For a long time her absence did not cause me pain although, as I realize today, I did miss her. Unaware of this, I did not miss her at the time, just as a sick person doesn't miss his health when a disease whose symptoms are not perceptible is at work in his body. I even felt a certain, shall I say, moralistic relief after the constant irritation ceased which Martha's different standards had caused. Especially as they had originally—at least in part—been mine as well, but which I recently had opposed as irritating, indeed dangerous for my day-to-day life. I left the world of mystery into which Martha, up to that point, had always withdrawn.

But I only seemed to leave it. After two or three years something within began to oppress me, something that was neither desire, nor longing, nor pain, nor illness; it was like a nothingness that had become independent and always aroused memories of Martha when it stirred, so that this nothingness slowly assumed Martha's contours in my imagination and became a photographic negative within me. My conception of another being inside me went so far that I thought there was no room left for my organs. I began to have stomach cramps, palpitations and difficulty breathing; when the sun suddenly disappeared behind a cloud, I was more inclined to think I was going blind than to look for a natural explanation outside of myself. In fact my gall bladder, stomach and kidneys soon showed lesions, which appeared so suddenly and simultaneously that they remained a mystery to my doctors. Several organs were removed, but my body didn't heal. When I was allowed a breather in the hospital, I spent most of the time sleeping, and I slept in order to dream. I lost that strange something within me; it fused with my weakened, unresisting body to become an individual once again wholly myself. Illness became the condition I longed for.

She asked herself whether, if she hadn't offered such resistance to being born, she would have found a way out—or if not a way out, at least a detour—other than that of turning herself into an immobile shell; whether, with more natural joy in living than she was granted, she would have made decisions at earlier points or crossroads in her life that would have spared her this present situation.

A life with Bruno, she thought, a life with Bruno could have been a way out. But she had left Bruno. At a certain, indefinable point before he had packed his medium-sized travel bag, put his key on the table and slammed the door behind him not loudly but distinctly, she had already withdrawn behind a wall of mistrust and suspicion, out of his reach, deaf to his protestations that she was suspecting him unjustly. She felt threatened by Bruno. Bruno had come into the world supplied with many talents, but his vocation remained a secret to him while he awaited illumination. None of his talents proved strong enough with respect to the others to justify preferential treatment or even neglect of all the others in its favor. According to Bruno, he had pursued his studies with success but no enthusiasm after he had decided, on the basis of tactical considerations, in favor of mathematics because he thought it immune to every doctrine—an opinion he had already revised by the time they met. In the final analysis, the relationship to computers is no less doctrinaire than the relationship to God, Bruno said: either you believe in it or you don't. Bruno believed in nothing. He also believed in no one, which kept him from being disappointed by anyone: he expected nothing from anybody, an advantage that won him praise on all sides for his tolerance and understanding, although Rosalind regarded this as the most extreme form of misanthropy. Bruno considered human beings rather like plants, whose peculiarities and sensitivities he eagerly observed and let himself be fascinated by, while their motives held little interest for him. The fact that the Count carried out his work as treasurer for GESOV with the same passion with which he tracked down the enigma of an unknown word in classical Chinese; that he kept the card catalogue of the hundred members and their dues with anxious pedantry, meticulously noting changes of address, telephone numbers, and pay increases; that he got really angry when these changes came to his attention too late; all this sent Bruno into cheerful outbursts that often ended with tears in his eyes. Rosalind could never be sure if they were caused by Bruno's unfounded laughter or by his unacknowledged compassion. It would never have occurred to him to ask why the Count, who belonged to no other organizations or associations, took his position at GESOV so seriously, since Bruno thought that every seemingly logical answer was aimed only at satisfying a superficial need for causality, and therefore was more inclined to lead away from the truth than toward it. In addition, Bruno loved the Count's peculiar nature, since he felt sympathy for people in direct proportion to their peculiarities. Bruno would have found it presumptuous and indiscrete to search for the mental roots of the tics and whims the Count had specially developed to protect the nakedness of his soul; and indiscretions, if they overstepped his general pleasure in novelty, violated a person's invisible boundary of self-defense and were considered by Bruno to be among the most unpleasant human qualities. Similarly, Bruno found it bothersome when Rosalind tried to get to the bottom of his character or wanted him to tell her why he had given up the piano once and for all ten years earlier, why he had fallen in love with that woman or had left this one. She spent entire nights trying to lend meaning to Bruno's statements about his role, by drawing lines from one occurrence to another, equipped with her scanty knowledge of his soul and driven by an unremitting duty to self-knowledge. She offered motives for his past decisions like an old herb woman selling her charms. Bruno was astonished at her unswerving stubbornness, whose meaning eluded him and which, in his opinion, smacked of missionary zeal. Bruno seldom agreed with the interpretation Rosalind made of a biographical detail. Maybe, but I don't think so, he usually said. This left her, and even worse, himself in a state of static uncertainty.

Bruno had lived with two women before he met Rosalind; eight years with the first and seven with the second. In her nocturnal interrogations she dwelt on the motivations behind these relationships, trying to shed light on Bruno's relationship with herself, to women and to love affairs in general. But Bruno pretended to know nothing about them. It's absurd, he said, to talk of failed relationships; after all, you don't say someone's life is a failure when a person dies, and you don't call a play a failure simply because it comes to an end. A love is like an organism, Bruno said; it has a childhood, old age and death, only sometimes, very rarely, is a love so powerful that it outlasts a lifetime, and then people talk about it for centuries. Rosalind's views on love differed from Bruno's only in the opinion of its finiteness, which Bruno accepted as a law of nature. Rosalind regarded herself as a victim from the very beginning, and unlike Bruno, she looked for the causes and how to avoid them. Whenever she talked about what in Bruno's eyes was the inevitable end of their relationship, hoping that Bruno would elevate her to one of the legendary exceptions, Bruno would say: but Rosa, I love you, which to her was an utterly inadequate explanation, for she wanted to know exactly how long he would love her and under what conditions, whether he would stay with her if she lost both her legs. Bruno said yes, and she generously rejected this as unreasonable, though she promised at the same time, of course, to stay with Bruno should he lose his legs, to which Bruno said: Just wait and see.

Bruno had imposed the same restrictions on his emotional life that he did in the exercise of his talents. When he was certain that he would never be able to play the piano like Glenn Gould, never write like Laurence Sterne, never attain the greatness of an Einstein in physics or the philosophical insight of a Schopenhauer, he decided to limit his predilection for art to a professional but completely passive one, and to make commercial use of his other intellectual gifts only to the extent this was indispensable to live.

When Rosalind accused him of using his capabilities irresponsibly—for her, talent also meant the obligation to use it—Bruno struck his opera singer pose, inclined his head to one side and said in a tone meant to console Rosalind for her lack of understanding: but don't you know that I'm the last superfluous man, Rosa?

Rosalind's attitude toward this squandering of knowledge was like the hungry who watch banqueters discard food they tire of. And after being moved by Bruno's evasions into the nineteenth century, she would suddenly burst out in an uncontrollable rage that screamed out of her in the feminist's vocabulary of identity, self-realization, partnership, chauvinism. She accused Bruno of being a cynic, a snob by birth, a coward who like Rumpelstiltskin concealing his name, rubs his hands together and laughs in secret at the stupidity of others. It would not have mattered to Rosalind whom else Bruno was laughing about if she hadn't feared it could be her as well. The suspicion that Bruno might despise her had grown in her slowly, without his having given her a specific cause worth mentioning. It had become so omnipresent in their life together that sometimes a thoughtless sentence by Bruno, behind which Rosalind thought she detected contempt, sufficed to make her burst out in tears. He was helpless against such outbursts, and every attempt to calm her was doomed to failure as Rosalind's suspicion was based less on injuries suffered than on the deep conviction of being contemptible in his eyes. Bruno's mere existence sufficed to cause her doubt—the unadmitted doubt as to whether her daily ambitions at Barabas' institute, her stubborn struggle for an argument or a wording important to her because she considered it the clearest proof of her sincerity—to crawl out of the corner to which Rosalind had banished it and to confront her disguised as any sentence from Bruno's mouth.

Perhaps it would have been possible with you, I say to Bruno, still sitting at the table though I hadn't been able to locate him a while ago.

Ah, Rosa, Bruno says, as he struggles to close his eyelids over his red and moist tired eyes, ah, Rosa, you didn't want to bear your shame. *Exegi monumentum aere perennius*...who wants to say that about himself these days. We all live in a state of shame. Bruno leans back, looks me over with his drunken eyes and turns back to his beer with a resigned shrug of his shoulders. But you don't believe me, he said. Everyone here think's I'm an idiot. Einstein. Einstein said that everyone here thinks I'm an idiot. Don't look at me like that, Rosa, as if I were an impostor just because I think you think I'm an idiot. The old man doesn't play dice, by which he meant the Lord God, and then he recommended the atom bomb to President Roosevelt, against the Nazis of course, and then it fell on Japan. *Exegi monumentum aere perennius*..., he regretted it later. Only Rosalind Polkowski with the Burgundian pride does not want to accept shame, she simply turns it down like a proposal of marriage.

It wasn't mine, I say.

It isn't mine either, Bruno says, it's yours, Count, did you lose the shame that no one wants?

Oh, oh, the Count says, apparently happy at Bruno's invitation to talk, and obligingly brings his beer glass over to our table.

Bad, bad, bad. He sits down close to Bruno and whispers: I'll tell it to you, only to you, Brünoh, I've lost the most important word. Sought, found, lost. The slip of paper is gone, somewhere between the pages of a book, and my memory, Brünoh, Paradise Lost, you know what I mean. Five years, ah, what am I saying, ten years work, I won't have the strength to look for it again, what a loss, and the shame, Brünoh, the shame.

Bruno clinks his beer glass with the Count's. Count, you

are an honorable man, you know how to bear up with your shame. If the world comes to an end you know your part in it: you have lost the word.

Cheers, the Count says, it's a good thing indeed that self-disembowelment for loss of honor has gone out of fashion. Even the Japanese gave up hara-kiri some time ago. One has learned to live with shame. However—I cannot help think-ing this—the ladies are finding it more difficult; too much honor was demanded of them in the past to be able to give it up that quickly, am I right, Madame Rosalie?

I do not want to offend the Count, so I limit my answer to a smile of feigned appreciation. As the waiter walks past I order three schnapps for myself in the hope that, freed from my sobriety, I can finally understand what shame the Count and Bruno are talking about. I keep my spontaneous thought to myself—that it's a dirty trick not to be able to take part in things for thousands of years just so we can now be hired as pack mules for the accumulated shame—knowing as I do Bruno's aversion to every theory that to him smacks of feminism, which he considers an expression of his respect for women. Women have been women as long as they have been humans, he says; in addition to a history as women they also have a history in the human race, and he prefers to see them as human beings.

Ah, Rosa, Bruno says and sadly shakes his head, aren't you going to have any mercy? Here we have brought shame into the world and no one wants to be its father, no one its mother, there are no brothers or sisters. It walks through the world an orphan, lonely and neglected. You know what will happen to something lonely and neglected? It will become base and mean, base and mean. Bruno drinks, probably so as not to succumb to his emotions, several sips of beer, one after the other. A rejected shame can turn into a homicidal bastard, Bruno says.

I gain courage by a perceptible increase in my mental powers thanks to the schnapps, and go on the offensive.

What about your shame? I ask Bruno.

My shame, Bruno says, my shame lives in a blissful state. When I notice that it's not doing too well I simply say to it: have a beer, why don't you? And it's happy again in a jif.

And what is your shame? I ask Bruno.

But Rosalind Polkowski, you ask me that, someone who was in league with it against me. My shame is that I don't do anything, Rosa, you know that. And it's your shame that you do something, you know that too.

I don't do anything anymore, I say.

Then you've added a second shame to the first, Bruno says.

The alcohol, I noticed to my satisfaction, was gradually carrying me to the heights of the Brunoic view of the world, so I ordered two more schnapps. Fine, I say to Bruno, I'll take it, and what does that prove?

Bruno laughs. Rosa's tendency to directness. Let's say you're no longer alone, it's always with you.

Do you know, Madame Rosalie, said the Count, that acquaintance with shame also grants some possibilities of consolation? He spoke in a conciliatory tone, for the Count was familiar with Bruno's drinking habits and was afraid that Bruno's already audible contentiousness could increase with alcohol and become directed against himself as well. Yes, consolation. Since they tore down the church in my home town and no Protestant protested, I avoid the center of town, especially the former Church Square, and prefer, even during heavy rainstorms, to take a detour. In a certain sense it's a gift to the church; afterwards, every time, I feel a little better.

I too have resolved to invent similar comforting pleasures for myself. Bruno suddenly grabs for my hand and looks at me with pity in his moist eyes. Poor Rosa, he says, perhaps you shouldn't have ordered them after all. Did you know, Count, that for Rosa good is good and evil evil? She always wanted so hard to be a good person. I want to be a rascal, and you, do you want to be a good person, Count?

Well, well, the Count says, a good person, horrible, nothing is worse than a good person. My father's side of the family is literally swarming with these good people. My father's cousin, an ugly old hag incidentally, was an especially good person. The moment she heard that someone had cancer or was on their deathbed she went there—she travelled three hundred miles to see a person die, out of pure goodness. Her greatest joy came when she was allowed once to go along to the morgue with a neighbor whose husband had been run over by a train. Bad, bad, bad.

The wonderful thing about Rosa, Bruno says, is that she doesn't manage to be a good person because she finds it so boring. This is also why the Church doesn't want the kingdom of heaven on earth, so that things on earth can stay interesting.

Quite right, quite right, the Count says and laughs in agreement.

Bruno places both hands on my shoulders and tries to straighten out his eyes so he can give me a searching glance. But Rosa, perhaps you aren't Rosa anymore when you stop wanting to be a good person?

Ah, I say, if you look at it that way I stopped being Rosa long ago. I've given up living like a human being. I'm nothing but a brain now, and as a brain pure goodness is not at all tolerable; on the other hand, the ill nature of a brain has no consequences so long as it doesn't have human helpers. Besides, I'm not at all sure I wanted to be a good person or if I only wanted the others to think I was. I would really rather have liked to have been able to lie and steal like Martha.

*

The room lay dark, its dullness broken only by the inert light of a street lamp, which Rosalind imagined to be a huge, omnipresent black funnel that swallowed and muted every sound to silence along the course of its infinitely tapered neck. It was so quiet that Rosalind could hear the blood coursing through her veins. So it's still alive, she thought, it's still alive, like a strange animal inside of me, and is resisting. For a few minutes she thought she could also distinctly feel the blood in her legs, in each toe, then again through her calves and thighs up to her stomach. It is resisting because it doesn't want to vegetate slavishly as the necessary evil of a brain, she thought. But it's too late, you are resisting too late, you weren't passionate and eager enough to challenge the brain's claim to absolute rule. Clairchen must have had a different, a wilder blood; and Martha too must have had a blood that had to rebel against the training that made her head afraid of bursting like an overripe melon, making it forget all other fears: the fear of not knowing what will come tomorrow, the fear of punishment, of pain, the fear of being alone, even the fear of dying.

I'm not saying that you were afraid or, much less, cowardly; you simply wanted too little. If you had once insisted, just once, on stealing or walking up and down at the Oranienburg Gate until some man came along who wanted to do it for money; if you had forced me to complain about the police in public or rob a newsstand, they might have locked me up, and after that nothing would have stayed the way it was before. Instead, you even allowed my brain to leave Bruno. Why didn't you flow seething and boiling into my arms and legs to force them to cling fast to Bruno, to grab hold of him and to defend him as an animal does its prey. You always kept silent or were afraid when I wanted you to tell me which decision to take, while my brain called in its dogmas, rules of behavior and precautionary measures to protect the given order the way a general commands his divisions. It had learned this all too well, Rosalind thought. As a child her body and mind had lived on the best of terms with each other, and never was the brain sad without the body being sad as well. When Rosalind was unhappy she confined herself to eating bread and water, took the sheets off her bed and slept on the bare mattress to support the notion of being the prisoner of imaginary enemies who appeared—coming as they did mostly from Rosalind's readings at the time—as witches, evil stepmothers or enemies of the Revolution. In any case, however, her misfortune needed an external counterpart: Rosalind's body obliged by cheerfully doing without amenities.

It was impossible after the fact to discover how and when this agreement had been lost, later even turning into its opposite; to say what or who had denied her body the participation in joy and happiness she was granted as a child, whether it was the adult's or Rosalind's own experience which taught her shame out of fear of being ridiculous and required self-control from her body instead of wild aerial leaps and spontaneous joyful dances. Rosalind, however, believed that the loss of the common joy of mind and body must have preceded that of their loss of common sadness. The change took place silently, the seemingly natural consequence of growing up. The brain began to mistrust the body, it accused it of being ugly and undependable; it denied it by carefully covering its nakedness even in summer, not even allowing bare arms to be seen by strangers. The body revolted in illness against the imposed lack of freedom, or, as soon as the tired or intoxicated brain slackened in attention, took revenge with unpredictable outbursts that brought nothing but sterner supervision. The impulses from body and brain to a third being within her, which Rosalind was inclined to call soul, were so disparate that Rosalind often believed she would have to divide herself in two if she were not to go mad. When she lay next to Bruno she wished to be nothing more than a body without a brain that knew and was aware of nothing beyond its own brazen animal lust to mate, while, at the same time, she watched in astonishment as her legs moved, her breath grew quicker, felt the saliva gather in her mouth. Rosalind's domineering brain tried to moderate the resigned and submissive activities of her body until it paused in shame and acquiesced to the brain, defeated by nature or habit. If her body was successful—which was rare—in escaping this control and forcing the brain to do its bidding, forgetting its shame and having no higher desire than conquest, Rosalind fell into a deep confusion lasting for hours, sometimes days. As if infected by a disease, her brain then lingered in the unaccustomed pleasure of having only to remind her body of touches and ecstasies, so much in harmony with the body that no other thought Rosalind was able to form could interrupt the game. Even when her brain slowly began to free itself from the union, it still clung for a while to the yielding nature of the body, inclined to masochistic feelings that deprived it of all the security and aggression peculiar to it.

Rosalind, who was employed at the Barabas institute as a brain to change the world according to the eleventh Feuerbach Thesis of Karl Marx, then became unfit for the work she was supposed to perform. In the end, however, the brain won out and alerted by this kind of surprise, offered the body fewer and fewer opportunities to repeat such escapades as threatened the brain's existence.

Hey, Rosi, Clairchen says and throws herself on the sofa with a groan; she coughs so hard her whole body shakes, just like when she was alive. Got a butt? she asks, and grabs for the pack of cigarettes on the table. Hey, Rosi, stop bitchin and be glad ya don't have to keep an eye out a my two tons a blubber, you'd have to be a Hydra at least to swing this, and you'd need damn good luck not to run into Hercules. Ya know wat happens to yer noggin when all that meat gets movin? It grunts an groans til yer brain konks out: total konk-out. The brain's the same, but ya got double the meat. That's why people're shit-scared a fatties—by instinct—'cause the ratio a brain and body is out a whack ya see. Either they can't get the blubber to budge or can't get it to think, like me. I couldn't get it to see reason, and my brain ain't got much more to do than get dragged around an wait for the right time to strangle this out a control hulk, the rest along with it a course, but there just ain't no other way.

There must be a way of living in harmony with yourself other than hanging from a chestnut tree or sawing off a leg, I say.

Live in harmony with yourself: ha, ha, very funny. Clairchen's attempt at laughter dies in another fit of coughing. I could a laughed myself to death over yer harmony, she says, and wipes the saliva from her mouth, sorry to say my throat ain't moist enough to do it.

It's in the fridge, I say.

Clairchen trudges along the thirty feet of hallway into the kitchen, takes all bottles out of the fridge that might contain alcohol, including the last bottle of sloe wine left me by my late Aunt Ida. That's for you, she says and takes a sip from the vodka bottle. Whadaya mean: live in harmony with yerself? I used to know a girl who ran from one shrink to the next lookin for her lost identity, till they found out she was average goodlookin, had average talents an average smarts. Right now she's in the looney bin; she thinks she's Brigitte Bardot, and that she's young, a course, and is a hundred percent in harmony with herself.

Martha was at harmony with herself, I say.

Clairchen crosses her legs, pushing her skirt way up over her fat knees, and I notice, inadvertently, that once again she has no underwear on. Clairchen enjoys sports, despite her corpulence, and did a cartwheel one Sunday in the middle of the pedestrians in Pankow Palace park, without it ever crossing her mind that she was naked underneath her skirt. After that I stopped being seen with her on the street without first making sure her clothes were in order.

Martha was at five-mony or six-mony or even more, Clairchen says; either way it never occurred to her to live in harmony with herself, which spared her from havin to feel like two. D'ya know I went streetwalkin with Martha one night 'cause she had to know what it's like? In Leipzig, at the trade fair, it's okay then. Martha even got one who paid in Western scratch; I only got one who had GDR marks. All of a sudden Clairchen opens her swollen, drunken eyes wide, points to the rear corner of the room and whispers: Hey, Rosi, who are they?

Third Interlude

The man in the red uniform:

Ladies and gentlemen. As Commissioner of the State
Authority for Psychological Control, I will now expound
several problems of personality, identity, identity crises,
identity cards and identity checks. This requires absolute
honesty on your parts. Money troubles, bowel
movements, sexual intercourse, all of this out in the open,
you understand. Who is who, the crucial question, also
of paramount interest in capitalist circles, as can be
deduced from the annual editions of the great work of
identity *Who's Who*. Who is who—the most important
prerequisite for the essential questions of our time: who
does what with whom. So let us begin. Who are you,
let's proceed one after the other.

The woman with a mind of her own:

Now wait a minute, do you think I'm crazy? I'm not
the least bit crazy. No one has to tell me who I am, I've
got a mind completely my own: one hundred percent.
Yessir.

She takes her identity card out of her purse and reads:

Dora Ottilie Friederike S., born March 13, 1935, in
Berlin, married. That's me, and I am identical with her,
too. There, you can see I'm perfectly normal. The fellow
here with his childhood, now he might not be perfectly
normal, I'm not sure he even knows who he is.

The man with the bloody nose:

The worst damned fellow to be sure, near or far, is the
foul liar. That goes for women, too, by the way.

The woman with a mind of her own:

Well, there you have it, Mister Inspector, you can't even

state your own opinion here, can't even help out your neighbor. If he doesn't know who he is, you simply have to tell him, don't you?

The man with the red uniform:

Quite right, but who's going to tell him? The question arises: who tells whom? And the answer is: I'll do it. Why? Because my office knows what is good for society. And as Marx quite correctly wrote, everything that is good for all is all the much better for the individual, which brings us much closer to solving the problem of identity.

The man with the unhappy childhood:

May I be permitted to make a proposal? I propose we begin by clarifying the term. Are we talking about concrete or abstract identity, about $A = A$ or about $x = y$ or about $x \equiv y =_{\text{Def}} \forall (P) [P(x) \longleftrightarrow P(y)]$, in which $\equiv$ is the relationship of identity, $\longleftrightarrow$ is equivalence and $\forall$ the universal quantifier. Let us refer to Heraclitus, to Parmenides, Aristotle, Schelling, Hegel, Leibnitz or Marx. Could we please begin by clarifying that?

The woman with a mind of her own:

That's just what we were waiting for: doesn't even know who he is and struts around with his little bit of knowledge gleaned at our expense, instead of being grateful for it. But don't get the idea I'm going to let you make an idiot out of me; I still know who I am.

The woman with the high voice: .

A or Y, what sophistry. *Man should be noble, helpful and good,* that's what Aunt Friedl wrote in my poetry album when I was still a little girl. And I've always tried to live up to it. And then Papa left us. Since then I've only been half a person. Child, you're just not yourself anymore, my mommy said to me just now. I'm a strong person only when I am with the family.

The woman with the delicate nature:

You simply should have emancipated yourself from your Papa. I tell Piti that all the time: Piti, I have to realize myself now in order to find my identity. If I don't I'll never be emancipated. You should have realized yourself.

The man in the red uniform:

We are coming now to the crises of identity, which manifest themselves in, may I have your attention please, all-encompassing and constant dissatisfaction, whose cause the divided person seeks not in himself but in the environment, in his marital partner, in his job, even in the government. The divided person has a seditious mind and strives for changes, becoming dangerous to society and, in individual cases, even a criminal. This is because the divided person has foregone the identity assigned to him in order to vegetate as a man without a country, a man with a stateless soul. He is the Wandering Jew.

The woman with the high voice weeps loudly into her hand-kerchief bordered with pale violet lace:

Oh, my heavens, why did Papa leave me? The poor children. I want so much to have my identity back.

The woman with a mind of her own:

Don't you have ears in your head? Be content—then and only then will you regain your identity.

The woman with the high voice cries louder.

The man with the bloody nose:

Your simple-minded view of the world scares sensitive souls. Dear lady, he says to the woman with the high voice, what you lack are convictions; believe a man with decades of experience behind him.

He gingerly touches his nose to see whether it is bleeding.

Convictions help. Join a party, an association or a committee. Then you'll belong, and should you make the effort you will quickly become a valuable member or even an indispensable one, and you'll see that you'll soon regain your identity.

The man in the red uniform:

And content, quite right. The highest goal of my office is the identical contentment for all our people. All for one, one for all. Just think of the inspiring scene of victorious soccer teams. And what constitutes the strength of victorious soccer teams? Their proper conviction of having to win. The right convictions are the right way to happiness. I therefore conclude: the main purpose of the identity check is checking convictions. I conclude: convictions belong on the identity card along with the date of birth. I conclude: everyone has to have convictions; if not, he cannot communicate them to my office; and he has to have the right convictions so that he is not liable to punishment for not listing them or for knowingly making false statements about them.

The man with the sad childhood:

I beg your pardon, but what does one do if one has convictions that have changed over a lifetime? I am asking this only in the spirit of dialectics.

The woman with a mind of her own:

You do have to notify the police if you decide to spray your car a different color. That really isn't asking too much. I can tell everyone my convictions, there's nothing wrong with them.

The woman with the gentle nature:

Are special convictions permitted as well?
The man with the red uniform:

> If they are the right special convictions, why not? My
> office deals generously with this sort of thing.

Clairchen exhales, bored. She grabs her head with both hands
and takes it off. Underneath, a small transparent head appears,
at first no larger than a puppet's, which slowly expands, and
is suddenly filled with blood, takes on a yellowish-pink tinge
now looking as though it had once belonged to Garbo. As
soon as the head has reached normal size it honors Rosalind
by tiredly opening its eyes. Clairchen places her old head
on her lap like a cat and strokes its hair. Poor noggin, she
says, poor old noggin.

Clara, Rosalind says, she wants to say, but cannot find
her voice because of a choking in her throat. She coughs to
draw attention to herself.

Astonished, eh? Clairchen says with her world-famous,
finely formed mouth, and attaches a melancholy smile to the
two words.

Clara, is that you? Rosalind is finally able to ask.

Rosalind points at the Garbo head, which is rocking
strangely between Clairchen's shoulders, like a Sphinx's head
on its lion's body.

That's me, too, Clairchen says. Always was, just didn't
see it, nobody saw it, 'cause a me, voice an all the rest. If
it was just the face, oh man, I've had my fill of 'em, I'm
sick of all that.

Clairchen caresses the head on her knees, as the Garbo
head tosses the locks gently from its face. I just don't know
what to do 'cause the contents up here stays the same, ya
see. All I have to do is knock back a couple an start thinkin

careful about somethin or even to say somethin, an I screw up again an things are like always. Hold on, here comes something clever now, Clairchen says, supports her delicate head on both fists, chews on her lower lip, sinks her fingernails into the rosy skin of the Garbo cheeks and, in fact, within a few seconds she really looks like her old self again. She raises her head and says: Ready? Wanna know the clever thought I just had? Does the fifth commandment apply to the hangman, too? Clairchen says and breaks out in a roaring laugh distorted by coughing which trails away like the sound of a moving train.

*

Rosalind is learning to understand what a wall is. To this end she looks unremittingly at the walls surrounding her, with the exception of the wall with the window, which is not characteristic of her problem. Rosalind considers constant observation of an object a means of getting to know it. She will not strain herself or concentrate too much; she only has to look at it without interruption.

Knowledge takes place in four phases.

During the first phase she collects all the information she already knows about the object. In the second she mobilizes things previously known and since forgotten, during which observation she also notices several hidden qualities of her object. Phase three reveals what the object under examination could be in circumstances other than those at the moment. During the fourth, endless phase Rosalind concerns herself with what the object is not.

In the course of an afternoon, Rosalind discovers the following about the wall: A single wall that exists in no relationship to another single wall, is a partition. A system consisting of four walls and floor, which has no ceiling, is a hole. A room with four walls, a ceiling, floor and a door, which cannot be opened by the inhabitants of the room, is a prison cell. A room with windows and a door, which can be opened and closed at will from both sides, is a room. The wall can protect the observer or the observed. Walls separate one from the other; you can knock on a wall. The walls around Rosalind separate her from her neighbor, from the hallway, from the corridor and from the street. She thinks that she cannot do without any of them. The longer she observes her walls, the surer she becomes that walls are among the most important regulators of human life.

And now, Rosalind says, I'm going to put my head through the wall.

*

A man is walking along the street. Every day, in every kind of weather, he circles the quarter, taking steps only with his left foot, then moving the right up to the left, he puts the left forward again, and on he goes. At the height of his right thigh a lifeless hand dangles on a lifeless arm: useless flesh. The other hand holds a cane that supports him as he walks. The man used to be a ticket-taker on the No. 46 tram line, which connects Pankow with the city center. As a child Rosalind was sure the man had been a Nazi because he looked like what she thought a Nazi should look like. He was robust at the time, in his middle years, with healthy limbs, an ashen-pale face on drooping cheeks from which the chin visibly jutted out, arousing an impression of cruelty. Anyone he looked at with his cold eyes felt vaguely uneasy. He looked almost impassively at the things and people around him, but behind that, so it seemed to Rosalind, there was hidden something threatening which could break out any minute in laughter. The man now has only one eye. Where the other had been is a gaping sore, a sticky socket in which he only occasionally wears a glass eye. With his one eye he stares a yard ahead of his feet as he walks; in order to cross this distance he has to put his left foot ten times in front of his right and pull the right foot up to his left ten times, and he looks for cigarette butts. When he finds one he bends over faster than you would think he could, picks it up and hides it in his jacket pocket. He wears shoes with heels jutting out about an inch, shoes allotted to him by the home for the elderly where he lives. Rosalind thinks the man is two hundred years old. She thinks he is immortal. First the man was a Nazi, then a ticket-taker and now he is lame and one-eyed and collects butts. He walks and walks.

When Rosalind pushed her head through the wall it was night, filled with the damp-musty autumn air and an indefinite light that streamed together from sporadic windows, street lamps and the half moon. Rosalind was sure that the man, although the home for the elderly forbade its guests from going out at this hour, was making his rounds nearby, or would be sitting on a bench in the playground where he occasionally rested during the day. I'll approach him, she thought, this time I'll finally approach him. She found him on the front stoop of an apartment building in Kavalierstrasse, where he was sitting one-eyed and still, his lips firmly closed over his toothless jaws, trying to control his heavy breathing as Rosalind approached him. Good morning, she said, after she had thought over awhile what greeting to use, choosing *good morning* because of the silence that indicated a time between midnight and five o'clock. The old man did not answer; instead, he crept into his own shadow and lowered his head to his chest as if he could hide that way.

Would you like a cigarette? Rosalind asked, less timidly because of the man's fear. The thin shape twitched slightly.

Go ahead, take one, Rosalind said and ventured to come a few steps closer. She held the cigarettes toward him in her outstretched hand. The old man raised his head and looked greedily at the full pack, undecided whether to choose a cigarette or solitude. Then he grabbed for it. His knarled hand shot out of the darkness like a wounded hawk. It took an effort to grasp a cigarette with his stiff fingertips. He wanted to say thanks, but all that came out of his throat, unused to speech, was a hollow gurgle that reminded Rosalind of Poe's story in which a man who is hypnotized while dying and kept in a trance beyond the grave, says with an indescribably fearful voice: I am dead.

The old man took a deep drag on the cigarette without raising his head. It was the tenseness of his gaunt body which led her to conclude that he noticed Rosalind's presence. Suddenly he spat out an indignant sound and let her know with a feeble wave that she should be on her way.

I see you often. Don't you ever sleep? Rosalind asked quickly, in the mildly loquacious tone of someone who has had a few drinks. The old man grunted something incomprehensible, cleared his throat, said something else of which Rosalind thought she heard the words peas and beans, but which made no sense.

After peas and beans I get stomach pains. Can't sleep, the old man said louder, as if his voice had just tuned in to the right frequency, and as clearly as he was able to without teeth. Peas and beans all the time, twice a week peas and beans;

Tuesday peas and Thursday beans, or Tuesday beans and Thursday peas. Peas and beans, beans and peas. Each time he repeated the words peas and beans, the hate in his voice became stronger, especially when he pronounced the *s* in peas. Rosalind stood helpless in front of the man, frightened by his unexpected outburst, although she had suspected something of the fearful energy concealed in this mutilated body. I'm sorry, she said softly, which the old man answered with disgusting, scornful laughter that shook his body, so much that Rosalind thought she heard his bones crack. You'll get peas and beans too one day, he said, old people get peas and beans. Then he was still again, stared straight ahead with one eye and smoked.

May I, Rosalind said, and sat down next to him, although she was repelled by his ugliness and his smell. He gave no sign of assent or rejection, perhaps he was hoping for another cigarette. When you don't walk anymore, he said abruptly, you die. You have to keep on going, going all the time. And children are scared, everyone's scared when they see me. He laughed silently.

You used to scare me too when you were still a ticket-taker, Rosalind said.

Didn't have a ticket, huh? the old man said and raised the eyelid of his healthy eye.

I had a month's pass.

He made a gesture meaning no, you didn't.

At the time I thought you were a Nazi, Rosalind said casually, as if she had long since given up the suspicion as absurd, merely the figment of a child's imagination.

Yeah, sure, Nazi, the man said. I was young back then, sharp fellow, uniform. Emmi got hot right off when she saw it. The devil, ha, ha, she was hot after every parade. Kurt, the jerk, stayed with the Socialists; not me, not me. Bad times, bad times, all came out in the papers though, confessed everything, the criminal. Emmi had the hots for him. He was a genius, I tell you. But no dick, he ain't got no dick. It all came out, but the Jews shouldn't a been so pushy. Caretaker, pah! caretaker, I didn't report nobody. We was seduced. All came out in the papers. Later. That's the end of that dream. Beansanpeas, beansanpeas.

The old man's eye wandered aimlessly through the darkness as he spoke to himself. Foamy saliva collected at the corners of his mouth. Rosalind had a hard time understanding the sentences he chewed in his toothless mouth. Emmi died, right after the war, raped, abdominal fever. They shouldn't have killed Röhm. After this it seemed that the old man had used up his strength. He fell silent. Rosalind gave him a cigarette, which he took this time without a thank you.

A light flared in a window across the street. Rosalind felt grateful to the insomniac stranger whose unexpected signs of life had freed her from the fearful idea that the old man and she were the only people on earth bound together by fate. She hazarded another glance at the half of his face turned toward her, the one with the collapsed, festering eyesocket. A demented, half-rotten old man whose secret had vanished in the smoke of two cigarettes. He'll die tomorrow or the day after or a year from now. The management of the home for the elderly will pass on the news of his death as a free bed to the competent district authority and order a simple funeral.

A dog appeared silently from the darkness and stopped in front of the yard door cheerfully wagging its tail. It was runty and bandy-legged, which suggested that a dachshund had taken part in its procreation. Its tail, which turned upward in steep ringlets, recalled that of a pig, but probably came from a spitz, whereas the head suggested a German shepherd in its geneology. When Rosalind called, it approached her cautiously and let its head be petted, closing its eyes languorously for a while. All of a sudden a warm liquid squirted on Rosalind's hand. The dog sped away yelping while the old man let the rest of his piss run on the ground.

The old man laughed with his mouth wide open so that his toothless jaws became visible, moist and obscene like innards. What an ass, he said, lets somebody piss on her.

Rosalind jumped up, stood in front of the man, whose dick hug out of his trousers like a dried-up root. The piss on her hand burned as if she had put her hand into nettles. You pig, Rosalind said, you dirty old pisspot. Disgust was raging inside her and she couldn't find words for it. You smelly piece of shit, you muck heap, fascist, Nazi, no, not even that, not even enough for a real Nazi, yellow, filthy, fucking fellow traveler. The old man stood up and shuffled off silently in the direction of Becherstrasse; his left foot in front of his right, then the right pulled up to the left.

Martha loved train stations and empty hotel reception halls at night. She was as incapable of resisting her longing for them as she could do without food or drink. She would almost stop talking and listening, looking restless and nervous at the door as though she were expecting something long-desired to suddenly walk in. Her trance could last for minutes or even hours, and it always ended with: I have to go there today, are you coming along? Although I liked neither train stations nor empty hotel foyers, and felt threatened by the rootlessness which pervaded them, now and again I went along with Martha. We would take the subway to the East Railway

Station, walk up and down the platform where the international trains depart, or sit on a bench while departure and arrival stirred the emotions of those affected. The grey-black backdrop of the train station—desolate and too small to hold its own in an international city—took on life with an excessive passion normally seen only in films. Embraces, tears, oaths, up to that moment which drew Martha here, when the train began to move with a slight jolt, inexorably increasing the distance with every instant between those who traveled and those who stayed behind. Arms stretched out of the windows of the trains to those left hehind, who still took a few pointless steps after the train as if they really wanted to follow it, to hold it back, though they all—those fleeing and those remaining—had long since resigned themselves to the unavoidable separation and had hoped for an end to the painful farewells. Martha then entered a state of excitement, like the wild, handsome, white-plumed child in the Douanier Rousseau painting who rides in innocent wickedness over his mutilated victims already pecked to pieces by crows. The futile gesture when those departing grasped the void in order to grab one another, the going and remaining, finding each other again. The spectacle of uncontrolled joy and sorrow intoxicated her, Martha said; she exulted and grieved at the same time, and thought she grasped for a few moments the meaning of human life.

Martha's unabashed voyeurism seemed to me crude, almost blasphemous, even if I could not say what was being blasphemed. There were times, nonetheless, when I too felt drawn into the giddiness of others, which touched my own hidden passions and plunged me into distress often ending in tears.

Martha said that bad drama was to blame for my collapses.

Luckily, she said, the professor had explained to her in time how she could attain outside the theater that Aristotelian state of catharsis without which man cannot know the variety and depth of his feelings. People used to go to plays to expose themselves for a few hours to a catastrophe which—heaven forbid—they wanted to be spared in their real lives. And while they wept at a great, dignified calamity, they wept also for their tiny one, which became, in a certain sense, ennobled through it. Once drama had renounced illusion and placed logical consistency before imagination and analysis before wonder, the theater had become an utterly stupid, foolish, nonsensical institution, which, the professor said, he found mostly boring. For what else should theater be if not illusion, as it is not reality when you come right down to it, the professor said. Reality was preferable in any case to a theater which wanted to affect reason more strongly than the emotions, because this kind of reality seems fortuitous; it was purely and simply the effect.

There are times in life when nothing happens, Martha said, when feelings shrivel or even die if they do not retire, temporarily of course, to a parasitic existence. Even the professor would sneak into schools at age forty to attend German classes. It wasn't until he became a pirate that he had real experiences and could do without school.

I'd like an earthquake, I said.

Because you know there's none on the way, Martha said. You have to ask for something mundane. There are train departures every day. Maybe you need burials or church services. People have the strangest natures.

Although I promised Martha to think up a suitable training program for my emotions, I still thought there was enough going on in my day-to-day life to protect me from apathy.

The uncontrolled and confusing collapses I had been through once or twice during our nocturnal visits to the station embarrassed me. I feared they expressed an inclination to hysteria, and in order to avoid such attacks I began to shun situations that might encourage them. After that, however, I was unable to enter a train station without thinking of Martha; an association that grew even stronger once Martha had disappeared, because I was convinced that she must have set out by train. One night, when she was watching the spectacle of farewell and departure, as she had done a hundred times before, she had let herself be carried away by the current, secretly, invisibly, without a goal.

The uneven, shuffling steps of the old man subsided into the stillness. There he is again, walking and walking, Rosalind thought, as she used damp leaves to clean her hand, which still burned with his piss. She then followed his steps to Becherstrasse, where he turned left and Rosalind turned right, in the direction of Berliner Strasse, which led downtown and to the East Railway Station.

Away from here, Rosalind thought, away from the old man and the stench that pursued her. I have to go to the train station; the goal was so clear and obvious that she didn't understand why she hadn't thought of it before. She had to go to the platform for international trains, and this once, not exclude herself from the passion out of fear of the confusion it could create in her; but to surrender herself to it, as Martha had done, to follow it and be seduced by it in whatever direction it led, to let herself be pulled along like Martha. She ran, pursued by the sound of her own footsteps, straight ahead, past the police station to the cinema. At the Vinetastrasse subway station she looked right, to Tiroler Strasse where Ida had had her last apartment. A small apartment with one room, kitchen and bathroom, built during the fifties for single people like Ida. Only women lived in Ida's building, the youngest of them was sixty-six, the oldest eighty-one. They took up a collection to buy a wreath for Ida's burial. In gold letters on a white streamer it read: To our dear Ida, our last respects. The household committee. When they laid the wreath on the ground where Ida was buried, the apartment still smelled of Ida. Her perfume blended with the seasonings, detergent, soaps and the scent of her body. The apartment still held the gestures with which Aunt Ida had placed things according to her idea of order and beauty. The dozens of small objects, now deprived of the inner meaning created for them by her memories, stood ridiculously on the shelves of the polished cupboard units along the wall. It was Rosalind's responsibility to empty Ida's apartment, to destroy it, to relinquish it, as Ida had been given up to her coffin. She had to carry out Ida's second death; she, the bureaucratic trustee of living death, had to erase Ida from the world.

There was a small pillow in a white ruffled case lying on top of the red cushions on the sofa. At the lower end, neatly folded, was her woolen blanket. Next to it on the table were her glasses and the last book Ida had read, everything as it was when Ida needed it before she was taken to the hospital for the last time. Rosalind sat down in a chair without taking off her coat. She did not dare use the sofa she was accustomed to sit on during her visits. She smoked a cigarette; the blue glass ashtray on the table was clean. The grandfather clock in the cupboard showed the correct time; it was quartz and didn't need to be wound. This last bit of Ida surrounded Rosalind like an illusion, like something that should not be. The room was bewitched, like a nightmare in which Ida's soul roamed at this hour. Rosalind felt herself to be part of a dispassionate atrocity. Today she was the perpetrator, at some later point she too would be its inescapable victim. I clearly remember the tension that affected me more and more violently the longer I sat in the room. Whereas a near reverence prevented me from obliterating every trace of Ida once and for all, something strange and angry slowly awoke in me and rose coldly in my throat, froze my jaw and increased my heartbeat. My hands turned cold and blue. Although it was warm in the room, I was overcome by a slight shiver and profuse sweating. I jumped up, lurched at Ida's sickbed, threw pillows and blankets to the floor, pulled the drawers out of the bureau, wrenched bed sheets, hand towels, stockings out of it and threw them wildly around the room, swept vases and figurines together on the display case shelves, tore the table cloth from the table along with ashtray, book, glasses and all. Destroy, I thought, destroy, destroy Ida's order, drive out Ida's spirit; Ida is dead, only her things live. I raged through the small room out of breath until I had undone all of Ida's work and had obliterated her order. With a bottle of wine I had found in the pantry, I sat down among Ida's shards now stripped of meaning, and I was gradually filled with calm. Yes, I was content. Never before had I felt a deeper harmony with a room. Never before had any order echoed my inner state so faithfully as this self-created chaos. Nothing, it seemed to me, sheltered as much hope as the desolation of destruction, and my mourning for Ida was displaced by a spiteful presumption, the desire to destroy in advance what would be left of me, instead of waiting like Ida until the things had outlived the person. To destroy the things and go on living, I thought, somehow, in another way, differently, in a way still to be seen. I sat until evening in the ruins of the apartment that had once belonged to Ida. Now, for a few weeks, it would be a no-man's land in which neither my nor anyone else's order applied. I felt free and lost, and when I finally began to cry, I thought I was crying for Ida.

The next morning, like every other weekday, she got up at six o'clock, left her apartment at five past seven and took the streetcar to Schiffbauerdamm. She glanced up Tiroler Strasse, to the windows of Ida's apartment on the third floor, and thought of the previous afternoon, not as a real experience, but as a scene in a film or novel she had seen or read. And someone, probably Mrs Petri, had asked her how she had injured her leg. For no reason and without noticing it, she limped for the first time in her life.

Except for those in passing cars, Rosalind had seen no one since leaving the old man. The trees extended their halfbare branches like human arms, and when Rosalind stood still for an instant staring at one of the trees, she thought she could clearly make it out slowly grabbing for her. Either we were trees before we were born or we will become them once we die, Martha had said. And Clairchen had claimed to know with certainty that she was related to chestnut trees; she could even talk with them when no one was listening. Rosalind's relationship to trees was no less intimate, but was chiefly determined by fear. A beechwood forest in a gust of wind made her think she was surrounded by an army of hostile giants who slowly and inexorably would crush her. Mortally afraid, she ran out of the wood and would not calm down until she was safely away from it. Hey, Rosi, Yer actin like a cave woman, Clairchen had once said when they were looking for mushrooms at Liebnitz Lake, if ya can't gobble up nature you're afraid of it.

Rosalind crossed Wisbyerstrasse, the border between the

districts of Pankow and Prenzlauer Berg. In the reflection of a shop window she saw, about a hundred yards ahead, a figure reeling toward her. A drunk, she thought. She stayed clear of the building walls in order to avoid him. The figure pressed his hands against his head, and when they passed each other Rosalind saw blood seeping through the man's fingers. She continued walking, fast.

It seemed to her that every now and then, far away, bells were ringing. If she stood still to make sure, she heard nothing but the wind, the banging of a door, a subway train rattling from Schönhauser Allee to Bornholmer Strasse; but as soon as she resumed walking, the sounds again fused in a heavy, thunderous tolling.

Two men were running on the other side of the street, one of them was leaning heavily on the arm of the other. They've had a fight, Rosalind thought, the last one and the one with blood between his fingers have had a fight. She heard a pitiful whining and was surprised that it reached her all the way from the wounded man; now there was a second groan, very close to her, below her. She looked to the ground. There was an arched body in the doorway next to the greengrocer's. Rosalind crouched beside it. It was a woman. Can I help you? Rosalind said. The woman did not answer. Her blonde hair was stuck together with sweat or blood. Shall I help you? Rosalind said. Dazed, the woman groaned. Rosalind saw that she was very young, a girl, hardly more than a child. Her thin chest twitched beneath her drenched blouse. Rosalind ran to the subway station, found a telephone that worked. There's a girl lying on the ground here, she screamed, I think she's dying. 98 Schönhauser Alle, quickly, come quickly.

Where? the man from the rescue squad asked.

98 Schönhauser Allee.

Who?

I only found her. She's dying.

Who?

I just told you, I don't know her.

Where? Who? What? the man said. Now, let's do this the right way: who are you?

Rosalind Polkowski.

Are you a relative of the person involved in the accident?

I told you, I only found her.

And she is dying?

I think so.

So she's not. We have a large-scale emergency in progress. All of our vehicles are out on duty.

But don't you understand...

Stay where you are; if you leave the scene of the accident you will be liable to prosecution.

He hung up.

As Rosalind left the telephone booth she almost ran into two men running one behind the other and carrying an ashen-faced woman. Although the men had their heads down Rosalind saw that their faces were smeared with blood. They were walking as if in a trance and did not notice her. Rosalind leaned against the telephone booth, closed her eyes, opened them again, recognized the swaying backs of the men, the head of the woman hanging to one side. No matter how many times she closed her eyes and opened them again, she saw only this scene, slowly receding. She looked in the direction the three had come from, and saw a new horror: bleeding, numbed people, alone or in small groups, reeling silently toward her, many with looks of bewildered terror in their eyes. The dead or stricken lay on the sidewalks; some had been able to find refuge in entryways; blood, groans, no one spoke. New figures appeared from the darkness. The uninjured were fleeing, mercilessly walking over or past the lifeless bodies on the street. Rosalind was still leaning against the telephone booth, frozen with fear. The repulsively cold stench revived memories of that Sunday in February when she and her mother had looked for Ida among the ruins of the Neander Quarter. War, Rosalind thought, there's a war going on here, no fire, no smoke, but there's the smell of it. What had she gotten into? A delusion of her senses, an optical illusion, but weren't they really running, more and more of them, more and more? Rosalind felt that her body wanted to wrench itself free of fear, to flee into numbness. Stay here, don't be afraid, this is only the retinue of Danko the Hero. They are wandering over the dark earth in search of the sun in order to set it free. But where is Danko the Hero, who tore his heart from his breast, to light the way for them? He put his heart back in his breast and has run off. Danko, the traitor. They are now searching for someone else to tear out a heart for them. Rosa, Rosalind, Rosalind Polkowski, your heart, they want your heart. Someone reached into her chest, grasped her heart with rough hands to tear it out of her body. Too small, it would be of no use, he said, and let it go. When Rosalind came to herself again, she was lying out of breath with pain, next to the telephone booth. Get up and go. Her body followed the commands of her brain reluctantly. She struggled along to a side street with difficulty, found an open garage door through which she fled into a small inner courtyard half overgrown with grass. She lay down on the sparse lawn, grateful that she had escaped the sinister spectacle, whose meaning she did not want to fathom. She closed her eyes, forced herself to breathe calmly, but concentrated fearfully on not falling asleep. She could go back, she could at any point undo the path she had taken, reclaim her own thoughts and come to herself in her chair, surrounded by four protecting walls, justified by her legs unfit for walking. But she wouldn't get to the train station then, and she believed that was the only place to pick up Martha's trail. And why should she turn back? Had she really been in danger? It wasn't she who had been injured, she was only a witness to the injuries of others. Not even that. Fear of the victims had caused her to run away before she could have become a witness. Instead of going on to the place of the massacre, she had fainted from fear and had hidden. And it wasn't until she was in a safe hideaway where the damp grass cooled her brow, that her curiosity rekindled. She regretted not having found out whom the reeling figures had been fleeing and why they had been wounded. And gradually, her terror at the scene became a nervous frenzy whose origin Rosalind scarcely understood. She had experienced danger and lived through it. This aroused her tired senses to a state of combat readiness. The thought that she was very close to a place where a struggle was going on that would leave behind victors and vanquished, a struggle as yet undecided, in which perhaps only one person would be needed to determine the outcome, filled her with an uneasy excitement about her own actions. She grew heady at the danger she had just fled and which now—a dreadful black animal with twelve feet—shadowed and challenged her. It drew her back into the Schönhauser Allee to the fleeing and the dying. She wanted to follow them to the place of carnage.

When she opened her eyes and stood up, she noticed that two windows were lit in the basement of one wing of the building adjoining the courtyard. A woman was sitting in a sparsely furnished room with her back to the windows. In front of her a man was standing with a pale face and sad eyes. He was wearing jeans and a white shirt with sleeves rolled up to just below his elbows. He bent over the woman, supporting himself with his delicate fingers on the back of her chair. All that Rosalind could see of the woman was black hair and her narrow, very straight shoulders. Although I do not notice anything unusual about the scene at first, it does, however, communicate a tension between the two that compels me to stay and observe how the scene might continue. My curiosity is aroused mainly by the woman's narrow, taut back. Like a mysterious smell, whether pleasant or repellent, that recalls times gone by, her back is both familiar and troubling to me. I carefully approach the windows and discover that the left one is slightly open so that I can watch the two through one window while hearing them through the other.

Please, put on the water for tea, I hear the man say. I notice that he has a gentle, almost warmhearted voice.

Why? the woman asks.

What do you mean, why?

Why should I put on the water for tea?

Drinking tea is part of the rules, the man says. Then I hear the woman go through the room with small, firm steps. I dare not believe what my senses confirm: the hair, the back, the voice and now the steps belong to Martha. But Martha has been gone, disappeared, for ten years. Am in Spain, looking for my father. Martha. I walk on tiptoes from the left window to the right in order to view the woman's face when she comes back from the kitchen, where she is presumably preparing tea at this moment. The man is casually leafing through a pile of papers lying on the table; now and again he pulls a sheet out and, hastily reading it, throws it back with the rest. If it was Martha, if it were only Martha, I whisper. I want to force myself to think this sentence to the end, but my hope, founded on the wish for the woman behind the window to be Martha, does not fit into any sentence. She is like air. As soon as I catch her and lock her into a sentence, like air in a balloon, she takes on the form of the sentence, losing her own breath, and I myself can no longer recognize her. The woman is now stepping through the door. She is holding a tray in her hands with a teapot and two cups, and as she walks through the light of a lamp I can identify her exactly: the heavy eyelids over the dark eyes, the pale yellowish skin, the childlike fingers. Martha Mantel. The man looks up and says something. Then, for only two or three words, Martha's lips move. I am unable to hear what they are talking about, but I definitely sense a danger, which though meant only for Martha, causes my own muscles to tense involuntarily, my blood to pulsate to brain and organs, and the hairs of my underarms to stand up. Martha sits down again in the chair, her back toward me, and I imagine that I am standing at my own back. I switch to the left, the open window.

And why should I..., Martha says.

I know that the last words, the ones Martha did not utter, were: *have to be killed*. Although I don't know what the two have been arguing about, I am sure that it is *have to be killed*. Martha did not want to utter these words because they seemed to her to forecast her execution. And the man is already confirming my fears.

Why should I kill you, he says, didn't you receive the written notification? he was very serious now.

What written notification, I think, and Martha says, no, nothing, neither oral nor written.

Would you please excuse me for a moment, the man says, I have to make a phone call.

My God, maybe this is all a mistake, I think, and hear Martha say in the same instant: maybe this is all a mistake.

Perhaps, the man says and spells out Martha's name on the phone. Madagascar, Abel, Roger, Tango, Hotel, Abel. So many names for one name. Okay, he says, but hurry up, I have my next appointment at two p.m.

A chair is moved, cups and saucers rattle. Martha is pouring the tea now. The mistake is due to the mail, the man says. The letter was entered by us a week ago in our outgoing mail register. You will receive a copy immediately via our messenger. There will be no delays because this time is reserved for tea in any case.

What's the point of stopping for tea?

During this time we will convince you of your infraction, he says and looks sadly at Martha. Although I cannot see both of them, I know his look as surely as I know she is going to be killed, for I feel his fair glance directly, a glance often practised before the mirror. It knows its own effect. I quickly go to the right window and, from behind Martha's back, see the man lower his glance into Martha's eyes, and through her into mine. Martha feels threatened, and the calm that has imbued her up to now lies heavily on her heart. Before the man resumes I am again at the left window.

I am a leading member of the Association of Male Poets, he says.

So Martha's situation is hopeless. Had she been brought to a secret government department or something of the sort, she could try to prove herself innocent, to clear up the misunderstanding, or at least request a postponement in some other way. But these people are inexorable; he will kill her, that much is certain.

Please, don't get me wrong, he says to Martha, we are opposed to employing any kind of violence, but there are certain priorities. The greatest good of mankind is language.

Life, Martha says.

Language, he says, please do not interrupt me. I know your views on the subject; that's why I'm here. Well then, language. It is traditionally subject to too much violence for us to stand idly by when a new form of linguistic rape turns from an isolated phenomenon into an epidemic. Your attempts at writing are—to put it politely—among the most unabashed and presumptuous infractions, not only of established literary values but of good taste as well. Your slender *oeuvre* omits none of the possible violations. We have been able to ascertain romanticism, lyricism, pathos, self-pity, infantilism and chic feminist gibberish. Words like hope, longing, pain and suffering along with their appropriate adjectives are altogether over-represented. Language is not a gay meadow with flowers, Madame, where you can take an amorous stroll. It is a towering cliff, and the poet has to utilize the smallest footholds to climb it.

Everything you say may be true, Martha says, but in my opinion the punishment is a bit severe. Do I really have to die?

We have conferred for a long time on the matter, the man says. Originally, you will remember, we decided only on a ban on writing by the ladies, but too many of them didn't stick to it. Some women deceived us for decades; they masked themselves by marriage, honest professions, even with a dozen children, so that one day, when they thought our attention had slackened or they were protected by age, they began again where they had left off in their youth, unchastened even by the intervening years. They padded their strange

113

biographies so as to create a greater impression and, for some people, even became idols. The desired effect, a dependable literary abstinence, could be brought about only if the person in question was able by herself to draw the consequences of our argument and choose suicide. This encouraged us to make the decision for the rest.

The man's speeches excite me for no apparent reason. Although I have never felt the need—if one ignores several clumsy attempts during puberty—to express myself in literature, and although I found Martha's poems often strange and arcane, with what I considered at the time an extravagant naiveté, I now myself feel accused, as if I and not Martha had written them. I suddenly know the sources of the poems and why I had the right to compose them this and no other way. But something, perhaps the man's handsome, serious gaze, prevents me from producing that in my defense. Martha too remains silent. Through the righthand window I see the man get up, walk behind Martha, who sits stiff and tense, so that he blocks my view of her. He is standing between us, but it seems to me that he is standing right in the middle of me. He now places his hands on Martha's shoulders, which fold like wings under his touch. He kisses her neck. Martha inclines her head and I hope that he will kiss me again. It's always the same, I think, always the same. If he would just take his hands from her, if he would stop kissing her hair, she could think things over to defend herself or to escape. Martha leans her head on his open hand and gathers strength for a sentence. Don't say it, Martha, don't say it, you know it's the wrong one.

Scarcely am I standing at the left window when she says it anyway. I've tried so hard, Martha says.

The man laughs indulgently. I know that you are all very

hard-working, he says. We also avoid all brutality. If you will relax, it could even be the most beautiful hour of your life.

I hear Martha crying, and my face is also wet with tears. Oh, please, Martha says timidly, there are men too who write the most awful junk without having to die for it. The man gently leads Martha through the room to her bed, which lies in view of the left window, so that I can now hear and see them simultaneously.

Lie down, the man says. Be very calm, I will explain everything to you. Imagine a tower, he says, imagine a tower of huge dimensions and grandiose height, built over a period of two hundred years, row by row. Each generation has added its stones in meticulous order, mindful of the work of their forebears. One finds golden masonry next to limestone, piles of sand alongside lumps of silver, but the whole supports its weight. This is poetry, the spirit of mankind given a form, you see. What do you think would happen if someone suddenly wanted to add to the next row something made of one part as before and one part wind, sunbeams and sea foam? Nothing would be added to the great work except a wretched pile of debris, a useless base for posterity to build on. He sits next to Martha and takes her hand. Do you understand? he asks.

Yes, Martha whispers, because she fears that he might get angry should she contradict him, and take his hand away again.

He smiles. Very good, Martha, then you also understand why men who, as you say, have written the most awful junk, do not destroy the whole.

Yes, Martha says.

His eyes fix, as if on something frightening, and slowly

moisten as his nose turns red. He gasps for air.

Are you sick? Martha asks.

He wrenches his hand from her, reaches into his pocket and just manages to press the handkerchief against his mouth before a series of four sneezes shakes his entire body. Then he blows his nose with relish.

Finally freed from his touch in which she rested like a baby, Martha slowly stands up. Take the vase, I think, and Martha moves slowly, silently to the window where the slim glass vase stands. I breathe a sigh of relief. Stay where you are, Martha says and holds the vase toward the man like a cudgel. Keep your distance, better yet sit down. Our brain, Martha's and mine, is now functioning perfectly normally again.

Madame, you are becoming hysterical, the man says and sits down with his legs crossed—apparently in fear—on the edge of the bed. And do not forget, Madame, next to language, reason is the greatest good of mankind.

Cut the nonsense, tea time has been called off, the rules have been changed. And don't call me madame. It sounds like an obscenity.

My name is Heinrich, he says.

I know, Martha says, I know your poems, they are very beautiful.

Oh, please don't say that sort of thing, Heinrich says, one shouldn't write beautiful poems in times like these. A poem has to be like a sword, a bulldozer, a laser. A poem must divide what has to be divided, destroy what has to be destroyed, stab what has to be stabbed. It makes me unhappy for you to say that my poems are beautiful. Beauty is an anachronism. It has to be destroyed so that it does not cloud our view of the ugly and the evil.

Martha is still holding the vase in her hand, undecided what to do with it and with the gentle poet on her bed. She could throw him out. Go or I'll break the vase over your muddled head, and that would be the end of the nightmare. She could also strike him down; that would be self-defense, I could testify to that. But now that he is sitting quietly at a good distance from Martha, turning his fair gaze inward, I begin to hope they might let each other live.

Without taking the vase out of her hand, Martha says: Please explain that all to me again.

You are a remarkable woman, Heinrich says.

I was almost a remarkable corpse.

Oh, I love dead women. I can love only dead women, Heinrich says, and something doglike, imploring comes into his gaze. It seems that he would like to say more about his love for dead women, an opportunity Martha should seize upon in order to improve her still vulnerable situation. If he takes an interest in talking to her, he will forget his contract to kill her for a while. On the other hand, there is the danger that in a moment of garrulous weakness he might let slip a secret that he wanted to keep completely to himself. Then he will remember his contract all the more. Still she must try.

Martha puts on her deep voice so that she sounds like a room padded in black velvet, a crypt in which treasures are hidden, and says: Then you must have gone through something terrifying.

Heinrich's body relaxes as though a tormenting pain had been taken from him. Terrible, yes, one can look at it that way. It was good because it was so terrible. She was vengeful. She poured all her blood over me, to the last drop. Furtively, in the night, while I was asleep, she cut open her veins and then lay her arms around me. When I awoke I found myself in blood; it was all over me: on my eyes, in my mouth, between my legs. I thought it was my blood. I thought I was dead. Anyone who sheds so much blood has to die. Then I saw her. Pale and unstained by a single drop. Next to her I was a monster, a blood-smeared monster. She wanted that. The guilt was supposed to stick to me.

Heinrich lights a cigarette, looks around for an ashtray.

Don't get up, Martha says, and with the help of a clothes hanger she shoves a saucer at his feet. Go on, Martha says.

I took a shower, Heinrich says, and after that I called a doctor. I was alone with her for a while longer. She was more beautiful than she had ever been alive. A white shadow, black mist.

Horrible, Martha says with her voice of black velvet, it must have been shattering.

Heinrich takes a drag on his cigarette, and when he is very quiet, he says: That made me a poet.

I see, Martha says.

Yes, Heinrich says. She also wrote poems, most of them were bad. Not as bad as yours but bad as well. I had to rewrite them later. But you're more beautiful, Martha, you're as beautiful as if you were dead, Martha.

Heinrich spreads his arms and they become powerful black wings in which he wraps Martha before she can raise the vase to strike him. He sinks his lips into Martha's neck and a sharp, pointed pain pierces my neck. Martha, watch out, I scream. Then the wall closes over as if the windows had never existed.

Rosalind touched her neck where she had just felt the pain. Her fingertips ran over uninjured skin. Only a violent trembling, caused by the night-time cold or the last hours' excitement, shook her body. She felt sick, she may have had a fever; she was dreaming, even hallucinating. Or how else had she gotten to be between these strange walls which enclosed her ever tighter and tighter and which, as soon as she looked up, grew higher until the bit of grey-black sky in the patch of roofs was only as large as a matchbox. Where was Martha? Martha, where am I? When the sirens screamed the all-clear through the city, a handful of pale children quietly came out of the basement, crept into the courtyard and played hide-and-seek under the moon.

Stay where you are and don't you flee,
The enemy's here but you he can't see.

From Schönhauser Allee she heard the shrill ambulance sirens and slowly recalled how she had gotten here. When she walked from the gateway onto the street she was surrounded by the stinking fumes of war. How many more miles to the train station: four or five.

Too many, she said and once again found herself in her chair surrounded by the four white walls of her room. Her lame legs hung over the chair like clothes. Her back and neck hurt from sitting motionless for hours on end, fear is hard on my heels, she thought, and is chasing me around the neighborhood like a trained circus horse. She mustn't give up; she would only take a rest and then continue on to the train station. All the same she had seen mysterious things, whose meaning she could now ponder at her leisure. How did Martha get into that apartment in Prenzlauer Berg after she had been missing for ten years and, as Rosalind surmised, had long since been living in New York? There were no clues to support her supposition. All the same, Rosalind was convinced that Martha's journey from the East Railway Station to Spain had led from Algiers and Toronto to New York. It was also puzzling why Martha hadn't changed in all these years, why the woman whom Rosalind had recognized through the windows as Martha Mantel resembled in appearance, gait and voice the Martha she had seen for the last time when she broke a glass in two by circling its rim with her index finger. Perhaps she had witnessed a scene from the time before Martha's disappearance, and it had come to her only now, like pollen in the air. She thought of the Count during the still gloomy morning following his fiftieth birthday, when he was exhausted from the honors just bestowed on him. Looking at the dawn with his red eyes, a bit ashamed of the view it provided into his soul, he said: Oh, this secret of reminiscences. Up until a few years earlier, he said, he had taken every vacation with a group of friends. Together they hiked to the neighboring low mountain range, drank plenty of Czech beer and Polish vodka, and he had the welcome opportunity to use his foreign languages. With the years the group, in part due to divorces or love affairs, in part as a result of heart attacks and other distressing symptoms of old age, had become smaller and smaller, such that he was forced to spend his last vacation alone. He then realized, with pain, that he was unable to walk the paths alone that he had previously taken in company. Memories lay along the rocks of the mountain paths and hung in the forest like spirits, listening for the sound of his steps, waiting to assail him and to whisper their sad songs of loneliness and the nearness of death in his ears. Having walked almost every possible path during his long life, there remained very few not taken, almost none at all, for the years which lay ahead. Oh, this secret of reminiscences, the Count said once again, and sighed gently. Rosalind's thoughts on what to make of the Count's words in her own experiences were interrupted by a half-hearted knocking at the door. The door opened a crack, and the man with the unhappy childhood slipped in.

Excuse me, please, he whispered as he carefully closed the door; I didn't want to bother you under any circumstances, but the matter is unusually urgent. I wanted to warn you before, but you were not yet back from your excursion.

Rosalind gave him to understand by nodding her head that he should sit down, which he hesitantly did.

Please, the man with the unhappy childhood said, be careful, you have been observed and your behavior has been discussed, a discussion the other ladies and gentlemen are continuing at this moment. But before much longer they want to appear here to demand an explanation from you.

Just like them, Rosalind said, but there's no reason to get excited.

You should not, however, underestimate these ladies and gentlemen.

Good heavens, please stop whispering, Rosalind said. I granted these people the right of free speech, that's all, and even that is only for as long as I have the patience to put up with them.

They must have forgotten that, the man with the unhappy childhood said. He spoke the first two words *sotto voce*, and the rest of the sentence again in a whisper.

Are you always so afraid? Rosalind asked.

The man nodded. Yes, indeed, he said quietly, always. What's more, I'm always having to decide which of the various fears I should give priority to. Take my current situation: I'm afraid what might happen to you if they find you unprepared. But I'm also afraid of what the man in the red uniform will do to me if you lose the struggle and it becomes known that I warned you. Such cases demand my highest concentration to find out which of the possible fears is the greater. I then try to confront this fear by abandoning the lesser one. This is how I became a professor. The fear of submitting a bad paper drove me to uncommon achievement. For years I regarded my fears only as a handicap; later, after much experience, I learned to feel a certain gratitude for them. In this way, despite a strict Catholic upbringing, I've become an atheist out of fear of breaking God's commandments. Similarly I've not joined a political party for fear of violating any of the statutes in force. Do you know that my name is Hansjoachim Schmidt, Schmidt spelled with dt. My mother's maiden name is Schulz, and we lived in Müllerstrasse. Can you imagine my shock when I understood what that means. I was twelve at the time. Schmidt, born Schulz, from Müllerstrasse, that's a hard fate, which was fulfilled whenever I didn't set my entire strength against it. My wife's maiden name is Meier, Meier spelled with ei. My youth was soured by the fear of becoming the common, everyday Müllermeierschmidt I had been born. Oh, don't talk to me about the joys of being ordinary. She had driven out any desire for being that, you know what I'm talking about, at a very early age. Her mother's maiden name was von der Mühlen, which in the long run only goes to show there's a Müller somewhere in her ancestry. But she was convinced that, if not noble, at least ennobled blood flowed in her veins, which she tried to enlist against the Schulz and Schmidt inheritance. Schmidt then fell silent. He wound his long fingers around his crossed knees and froze in a complicated geometric figure with several acute angles.

You certainly do have a very respectable fear, Mr Schmidt, Rosalind said. I am largely unaware of the character of my own fear. I have simply observed that a situation very often produces equal degrees of fear and desire in me, in which I cannot fathom whether my desire frightens me, or whether both are appropriate and equal reactions to a single course of events. As long as I can remember, the thought of stealing something has always excited me. I walk between the shelves of a supermarket and imagine that instead of putting some object or other, a jar of jam or a bar of soap, into my shopping cart, I slip it into my pocket. My body immediately loses its indifference. It begins to glow and twitch in fevered excitement as my fear chases my desire in order to grab it before it reaches my hand. And my excitement is redoubled as the desire to steal becomes uncontrollable. This causes fear—but fear of what, since I am unobserved and need fear no consequences—to put in its last reserves and grab my greedy hand so firmly that I'm dripping with sweat.

Mr Schmidt cracked the joints of his intertwined thin fingers. Rosalind felt irritated and disgusted at the sound. Stop that, she snapped. He laid his hands obediently on his knees and began to breathe heavily and loudly through his nose instead.

What's the matter with you, Rosalind asked, don't you feel well? Oh, I do, Mr Schmidt said, his voice trembling with excitement. I was just thinking that I might get a di...The door popped open and, led by the man in the red uniform, the persons whom Mr Schmidt had called ladies and gentlemen entered the room, sat down with serious expressions, without saying hello, around Rosalind's table. Mr Schmidt whispered an inaudible excuse and left his place next to Rosalind so as not to attract attention, fearful as he was, and blended in with the others.

The man in the red uniform places a thin file on the table, moistens the tips of his right index finger and thumb, and begins to leaf through the file:

Since the members of the commission unfortunately, emphasis on *unfortunately*,

he looks up and glances sharply at the group, then continues:

have not yet, emphasis on *not yet*, come to a unanimous decision, we are continuing the deliberations on the Polkowski Case in the presence of the accused. The charges are illegal imagination, and its use, should it occur again.

The woman with the tender nature:

And I'm sticking to my guns. If you forbid Piti to use his imagination he…

The woman with a mind of her own:

Now don't be so stubborn. The Chairman doesn't mean to outlaw imagination as such, he simply wants to prohibit illegal imagination. Everything that's not permitted is prohibited. That's clear to everybody.

The man in the red uniform to the woman with the tender nature:

Whoever said I was against imagination? I am in favor of imagination; for a constructive, positive, clean imagination.

The woman with the high voice:

Oh, that's what Mommy always used to say: Child, beware of filthy imagination. Your imagination has to be as clear and pure as rock crystal, so you can see the world in its nicest colors, Mommy said.

The man with the bloody nose:

> If I may be allowed to contribute something to the deliberations: We should distinguish between active and passive imagination. Passive imagination can infect a person even against his or her own will and should therefore be judged with leniency. If Joan of Arc had not spread abroad to the world her talks with the archangels and if she had not, more importantly, translated her imagination into acts of war, no one would ever have tied her to the stake.

He gingerly pats his nose with a clean handkerchief; satisfied, he places it back in his pocket and says:

> First of all we want to find out whether Mrs Polkowski overstepped the boundary between a passive and an active imagination.

The man in the red uniform:

> Hear, hear! So you want to let the potential murderer dream about murder until he dares to commit the crime! The one who dreams about a crime today is tomorrow's criminal.

The woman with a mind of her own:

> Anyone who defends that sort of thing is guilty himself. That's perverse, that's what I think, yes indeed. Do you really think I have no imagination? A goulash without imagination, ha, what do you think that is? But it isn't imagination when you burn a goulash or when you figure out where to get wormy meat for one, because that's just perverse. But you don't call it perverse to rot our lives and our country. You call it imagination. Well, I'm against it.

The woman with the high voice:

> These poor people, perhaps one ought not be so hard

on them. How many times have I made up my mind to think of something nice. Then I sit down in the easychair Papa always liked to sit in, and want to think of what a happy family we were when Papa was still with us. And then I'm attacked by such terrible thoughts...that Papa may be at this very moment with another woman...

She sobs and is unable to continue talking.

The man with the unhappy childhood:

If I may be permitted a technical remark: it is impossible to abolish subtraction and retain addition, just as giving up division would necessarily mean the loss of multiplication. What I mean to say is that the elimination of the negative manifestation of an object automatically implies the elimination of its positive manifestation, and thereby the elimination of the object itself; if you will allow me this analogy.

The woman with a mind of her own:

Then keep your divisions or whatever they're called to yourself, why don't you; no one wants to talk about them anyway.

The man with the bloody nose holds his handkerchief in front of his face and does not speak.

The man in the red uniform:

Think of those men in responsible positions. For them, imagination means the firm belief in the good. What could they do without this faith? I dare not say what. However, being who they are, they believe, for the good of us all, unswervingly, in the love of the nation, in the health of the economy and in the power of persuasion of the press. Figure out for yourselves the high degree of responsible imagination which day in day out, hour after hour, these men, examples to us all, have to use.

I am also speaking from humble experience.

The woman with the tender nature:

But Piti is an artist. He had to be special because he would be average otherwise, and this is also why he needs a special imagination. He told me quite recently: Oh, Tipi, I just had a frightful vision, there weren't any trees left in the world anymore. And we were very happy, Piti and I, because that proves that Piti is a true artist.

The woman with a mind of her own:

Anyone can say that. I just had a vision that there were no more people, which means, I guess, that I'm an artist too. Your Piti would do better to think of a way to get the trees to grow again, but I suppose that's too hard for him.

The man with the bloody nose takes the handkerchief from his nose for an instant:

Art at home replaces the ax in the forest, ha, ha.

Everyone laughs except the man in the red uniform.

The man in the red uniform:

What's so funny? There's nothing funny about it. It's a matter of law and order. Of law and order in the brain. If the order of the brain isn't safe, the whole head is at risk. You see? For the head—that is, order—to be safe so that order—that is, the head—is orderly? The object is to make it compulsory to wear a thought-image-transmitter, TIT for short, which transmits every thought from the brain to a screen worn over the head so that secrets taking place in the foreseeable future are eliminated. Anyone who wants to keep a thought to himself must not think it, which guarantees the tremendous didactic effect of the apparatus from the outset.

Unchecked thoughts, like *I could kill him*, would immediately be shown on the screen as murder, in color, of course, and would permit the arrest and punishment of criminals before they commit their crimes. Unfortunately the TIT is still in the research and development stage, so we were forced to use conventional charges in the Polkowski case: forbidden contacts, incitement to rebellion, refusal of assistance, slander and so forth and so on.

The man in the red uniform jumps up, supports himself on the table with the palms of his hands, stretches the trunk of his body bolt upright like the trajectory of a cannon ball and screams:

Defendant Polkowski, what was your purpose in transforming the peaceful pedestrians of one of the main thoroughfares of the city into agitators and corpses?

Don't get excited, I think, don't answer. The man is wrong. He is my creation and has to obey me. He must have forgotten that. Or has he freed himself from me? By magic maybe, if I were afraid of him. Am I afraid of him? The man is standing in the same pose at my table, apparently without strain, and is staring unblinkingly at me. He wants an answer from me. I'm no longer sure he would follow my command to sit down and remain quiet were I to give it, so I hesitate. Mr Schmidt, the only one whom I might expect support from, is still sitting wedged in at an acute angle among the others, who, like him, stare silently into space. Only the woman with a mind of her own risks a canny look now and again in my direction to warn me. Her common sense seems to comprehend the weighty decision of the moment. I have to say something. What purpose did I have in mind; I had no purpose in mind. Really a strange word: purpose, purpose, to purpose. What I did was purposeless. I wanted to go to the train station, and these purposeless people approached me. There was no purpose, therefore I couldn't have followed one. What in heaven's name was that supposed to mean: a purpose? Please give me a pound of purpose, or do you say purposes; three purposes, please. Or: go to the next purpose, then turn left...I'm beginning to doubt whether this biting, angular word exists, whether it didn't fall on my head like a pointed stone where it is pressing and pricking me. Didn't Ida use it, more out of helplessness than malice, when she hit me with the carpet beater crying in a cracking, cooing voice and repeatedly wanting to know why I had climbed onto the roof? Did she simply ask why at the time, or did she, or so I believe, want in her perplexity to demand the purpose of such an unbelievable act. In the end it came to the same thing: why, for what reason. I had to let her beat me because I didn't know the answer. I could have given as a reason: that our house, once on top of it, didn't seem as incredibly large anymore; or, that the roof didn't have a pointed ridge as I had feared, but enough flat surface to walk around on. But I didn't know that until I got up there. We climbed onto the roof because we wanted to be on the roof, and there was no hidden purpose.

The man persists in his idiotic eagerness, now and then he loudly swallows his abundant saliva. For a while I think that I have been through exactly this scene before, have felt precisely the same helpless disgust at the man's drooling triumph. But the more desperately I try to remember, the more incredible it becomes, until the memory fades beyond where my senses can follow it. I am still silent, and although I try to defend myself, my certainty of not being guilty is vanishing. Where did the corpses come from, where did all that blood in my head come from? Perhaps I really am the culprit who thinks all this up; perhaps it's not my fear, but rather my bloodthirstiness that projects these images within me. When I open my mouth to confess my doubts, I am prevented from speaking by familiar laughter distorted by coughing.

Hey, Rosi, Clairchen says, ain't ya ever gonna wise up? She is floating, tripping gracefully on her toes around the furniture, her fleshy arms longingly stretched out in front of her as if she wanted to touch something that is forever pulling away from her. See how I can dance, she says and lets her bulky body rotate in a perfect pirouette, look what I can do. Clairchen extends her right leg vertically into the air so that her black silk ballet shoe strikes the ceiling lamp while she stands alternately on the sole and tip of her left foot. Ya know what I hated most in my life, Clairchen says, I couldn't dance ballet. I used to lie in bed for hours in the evenin, flipped on music in my head, usually Mozart, an looked at myself dance, like now, only I had more room then, of course. In the mornin I knew again for sure I couldn't do it, an then I sometimes just didn't wanna get up, 'cause I couldn't hack it. Clairchen leaps lightfooted into the air, revolves once around herself and lands safely next to my chair.

Clara, I say, you look very beautiful when you dance.

I know, Clairchen says, I seen myself often enough to know, but I'm the only one wants to believe it.

When she lets herself fall to the carpet, exhausted and huffing, those forgotten in the corner of the room applaud.

Bravo, the woman with the tender nature cries.

Fantastic, the woman with the high voice moans.

Even the man in the red uniform claps his short-fingered

hands.

Tell 'im 'e can sit down now, Clairchen says.

I tell him. And not seeming to know himself why he is standing, he obediently sits down at his place.

D'ya understand now? Clairchen says.

I'm grateful to Clairchen for the rescue, but I don't talk about it because it embarrasses me that I almost let them take me unawares, and because I'm vexed at her condescension toward my failure, the shaking of her head and the wiseacre smile.

Man, oh man, almost chops off her legs an keeps on with the same ol' bullshit. Imagination, Rosi, Clairchen says, somethin ventured nothin gained. She then gets up, gives me a firm pat on the shoulder: Don't forget, Rosi, imagination, she says again, and exits through the window with three sidesplits, without breaking the pane. Clara, Clairchen. Stay here! Come back, I call after her or think I have called, but Clairchen has long since faded into the impenetrable darkness of night, and Rosalind is left alone with her uninvited guests.

You can go, she said in a tired voice, for the last time, I've had enough of you. I will forget you, I will simply open the trap door in my right temple and plunge you into oblivion.

The figures did not move. Like lifeless puppets, with silly grins on their faces, they sat in their corner.

Beat it, we have nothing to do with one another anymore, Rosalind screamed, but they sat in mute harmony around the table, and Rosalind noticed that they were no longer breathing. They had petrified here in her apartment into a monument, a true-to-life tableau for a future folklore museum. She would have to live with them in the future and could not forget them so long as they were in the room. An unsettling thought, Rosalind found, but she comforted herself with the certainty that they could no longer harm her. All the same, she thought, she should have refused them entry in the first place or ignored them once they had forced their way in; she could have made an exception in Mr Schmidt's case even if he had shown himself to be weak and afraid. Mr Schmidt sat, immobile like the other five; he alone did not smile, but how could he, for he had never learned to smile. He stared ahead impassively but in earnest. Something about Mr Schmidt, a barely perceptible gleam in his eyes or a slightly trembling strand of hair, led Rosalind to address him softly. Mr Schmidt, Mr Schmidt with dt, she whispered, are you still alive?

A faint twitch passed over Mr Schmidt's face. Excuse me, he said, I must have fallen asleep, the excitement and a lack of sleep, I must have dozed off a bit.

After he had recovered from his numbness and had recognized the company he was in, he jumped up in horror. Oh, God, he mumbled, oh, God.

Go ahead and touch them, Rosalind said.

Mr Schmidt extended his boney index finger and cautiously poked at the chest of the man in the red uniform. Hard as stone, he said and shook his head anxiously, utterly incomprehensible from a scientific point of view.

Martha claimed, Rosalind said, that she learned from her pirate professor that all forgotten fairy tales fly through the centuries to fall somewhere to earth one day to catch you unawares for a few minutes or hours, even weeks and months for very long fairy tales. Most such captives believe they are the victims of an optical illusion. Others are said to be confined to mental institutions because they insisted, against all reason, that they really had witnessed the incredible. Martha said that such a descending fairy tale could suspend all natural laws, which leads me to believe that we won't be able to rid ourselves of these.

I can give it a try anyway, Mr Schmidt said and shoved his arms under the knees and armpits of the woman with the gentle nature. But he was unable to budge her a fraction of an inch. He suffered Rosalind's shaming glance at his thinness.

Doesn't matter, Rosalind said, I wanted to go to the train station anyway. I'll take you along, it would be best to come along.

Come along, Mr Schmidt whispered, yes indeed, go away, I should go away with you. Oh, how often have I planned to do that, to get up and go away, to have a look around once, perhaps even twice or three times, so as to enjoy the pleasures of setting out, and to go on. I was never able to do it, and I've often asked myself why I can't. I found no answer, perhaps because I never knew where I wanted to go; I need a goal, I need a goal for everything. But didn't you just say: to the train station? All right, to the train station, but afterward do you know where you want to go from the train station? You don't speak. You don't speak because you don't know. For years I've been tormented by a dream. I dream it only in the spring and the fall, never in summer or winter. That's odd, isn't it. I dream that the trains to the big cities run through my room, almost through my brow. My room is a tunnel through which the trains have to pass on their routes. No train has yet stopped to take me along. Sometimes travelers lean against the windows and poke their heads dangerously far outside the train, but they don't see me hidden in the darkness of the tunnel. Nor do they hear my cries. I don't cry anything specific, just meaningless screams in order to bear the noise of the trains. I seldom scream words.

Halt. Stop. I've even called for help although I know that no one will hear me. Or because I know that no one will hear me. And if one day one of the trains stopped in my room, in front of me, I would not get on. I would want to stand and watch it go past, like those that had passed before. I would want to stay behind. Step back from the edge of the plat-form! Stand back! That is meant for me. And then again I dream that I stare at the tracks, which run toward me with iron sternness, and I wish there were something there meant for me, the way into myself. But I don't want to bore you. No one's interested in other people's dreams. Only our own dreams can give us an inkling of our inscrutability because we alone know the reality that they reflect. The mystery lies in the difference, which only the dreamer can detect.

Mr Schmidt fell silent, as though resigned to the general futility of sharing one's innermost self with someone else.

Mr Schmidt, Rosalind said, Mr Schmidt, you have no idea how well I understand you and how familiar your vulnerability and your longing for a higher purpose are to me. If it weren't for that, I wouldn't be sitting here: I would be in Spain or New York with Martha. If it is true, however, what Martha and the professor said about falling fairy tales, then both of us are now in the midst of a fairy tale which suspends not only the laws of nature but human qualities as well. Your fear is no longer your real fear but only your memory of it. This is the chance to defeat it once and for all. Let us assume that you were now to do something for which you never had the courage: you steal or leave your wife, and then you observe that it was very easy, none of the things you feared happen. Your fear was unfounded.

And what if it does happen? Schmidt said, and cracked his knuckles.

It is a chance, Rosalind said, your chance. After a while she added: And mine, too.

Schmidt took off his glasses, carefully cleaned them with a specially designed chamois cloth, put them gently back on his nose, adjusted the fit of the bows with a practised gesture and directed his attentive gaze at Rosalind. Have you ever stopped to ask yourself why you have yet to kill a person? I've thought about it and have found out something horrifying: it's only out of fear that one day I would want to undo the killing that I have never killed. There is nothing I fear more than the irrevocable. I suppose that my bent for science arises from this fear, because science has no finality. Every bit of knowledge feeds the desire for more.

I knew a young man, Rosalind said—only in passing, he lived in the neighborhood—who at seventeen stabbed someone to death. He was quiet and inconspicious as a child, he lived alone with his mother. When she remarried she moved with the son to her new husband in P. I learned by coincidence that the boy had become a murderer. His grandmother had given him a little dog while he still lived in the city. But there must have been a Labrador in the mongrel's pedigree, for within a year the dog grew to be unusually large and ugly. The stepfather detested the animal and tolerated it only outside their small house. Both child and dog resisted the order, which angered the man even more since the dog obeyed only the boy. After an especially violent quarrel the man tied the lad to the pear tree in the garden behind the house and killed the dog in front of his eyes. The boy was twelve at the time. He became a quiet loner, had no friends until he fell in love with a fat girl generally regarded as ugly. Every time the couple showed up at the small town disco on weekends, the lad was laughed at for his girlfriend's ugliness. One day he threatened to kill the next person who provoked him. When he went to the disco with his girlfriend the next Saturday, he put a knife into the grip of his boot and stabbed the first one who ignored his threat. During the trial the dog's slaughter was brought up. The stepfather hanged himself in the basement of his house. When I heard the story a few years ago, I asked myself why I had never killed.

And? Mr Schmidt asked, curious.

I don't know, Rosalind said, it just may be that no one has done anything to me that would bring me to kill. Who knows? I tended to see the way out in my own death.

Oh, Mr Schmidt cried, excited, that should give you something to think about. I believe that thoughts of suicide often express a keenness to murder, simply rechanelled by moral scruples. One is ashamed of one's base appetites but doesn't want to sacrifice them and therefore dresses them up in garb that ennobles instead of degrades them. There are people who dwell on suicide for a lifetime without ever coming close to killing themselves. They die innumerable deaths in the imagination, and each time they verge on murder without having to admit it to themselves.

Mr Schmidt pulled at his long fingers and thumbs, cracking each after the other, until Rosalind felt ill.

Believe me, Mr Schmidt said, it is simply fear of the irrevocable, in your case as well. Even if you insist on having desired only your own death, you'll have to admit, after all, that you're still alive. With that, Mr Schmidt got up, went to the door, and turned around before opening it; I'm sorry, he whispered, but there's such a thing as human nature. He then left. She did not hold him back although it was in her power to do so, and she would have been happy for his company in what lay ahead. Even if the frightened Mr Schmidt could not have offered her any real support, his presence, even the obligation to protect him in an emergency, would have eased her burden of loneliness. But she was too exhausted to keep Mr Schmidt from leaving. A great deal had happened during these last days. Though Rosalind herself had invoked her experiences, had conjured them out of the darkness of her being into reality, she could hardly tolerate them. Hadn't she thought at first that she was the director of a great theater whose actors were subject to her will alone? She had wanted to let loose a chaos without rhyme or reason during the freedom that paralysis had granted her. Instead, she had become an actress herself, subject to the whims of her creatures, who paid as little heed to her as had their models during her previous life.

I mustn't stay here, she thought, I have to go, I have to leave this apartment for good.

*

Ida had already been buried three weeks when Rosalind carried out the last act of her obliteration. The man, a representative of the State Purchasing Office, stormed the apartment with quick, athletic steps, briefly gave Rosalind his wiry hand, entered the room ahead of her, scanned the objects he had come to view at seven o'clock in the morning with the cool gaze of a bird of prey, and then collapsed, a vexed smile on his mouth, onto one of the two armchairs.

I'm interested in the vases, he said, taking a form and a metal pen from a folder.

The vases were a present from Hans, the worker at the Royal Prussian Porcelain factory; they were never used, were carefully dusted every week, and, except for a few photos, were the only visible evidence of the six happiest years of Ida's life.

This is RPP, isn't it? the man asked, without casting a second glance at the three big-bellied containers with red, blue and yellow floral designs. It was a rhetorical question, meant as a sample of his expert knowledge.

Not the vases, Rosalind said.

Thought as much, the man said. Building number?

Rosalind didn't understand.

What is the number of this building?

Twenty-five.

The rest is trash, the man said, after he had entered the number on the form. He stood up and drummed his fingers nonchalantly against the side of the cabinet: At most five hundred.

That cost two thousand, Rosalind said.

He gave a short laugh. We get dozens of these every day. Five hundred, for your sake.

The man was at least six foot two. He used to be a swimming instructor, but had always been interested in antiques. He walked across the room in three strides, shaking his head either out of distress at Ida's poor taste or at the bad deal he was expected to make.

The armchairs are virtually new, Rosalind said.

Ida had bought them, when she was already deathly ill a year ago, as if life could somehow be entreated, as though someone who had invested in the future could not be denied the right to enjoy it. It had to be worth it. Being worth it was one of the most important criteria in Ida's life; and five years earlier, when she was still healthy, she had rejected the purchase of new armchairs precisely because she was too close to death. Only a few more years, it isn't worth it, she had said. Ida bought them between two stays in the hospital. She took what there was, black imitation leather with blue bouclé: awful and expensive.

A hundred each, the man said, that's the best I can offer.

I'm selling off Ida, Rosalind thought, but Ida is dead.

She followed the man into the kitchen.

People always think their junk is worth something, he lamented, but I don't get anything out of it if I cheat them. He opened the kitchen cupboard with a sigh. In good condition, but what use is it? That model is at least fifteen years old. He wrote numbers down on a sheet of paper. He looked at the mirror framed in wrought iron in the hallway with a helpless shrug of his shoulders. The very sight of it seemed to pain him.

When he looked at her, Rosalind felt the man's tortured grin reflected on her own face. She was laughing with him about Ida.

One thousand thirty marks, the man said, minus twenty percent commission.

He noted down Rosalind's account number. The things would be picked up on Tuesday, between six in the morning and five in the afternoon. He left in a hurry, the way he had come. Rosalind gave the key to the woman next door. She then left Ida's apartment for the last time.

*

The Schönhauser Allee spread out before her in its granite majesty like a fortress. No human being was to be seen. Nothing moved, even the last withered leaves on the trees hung motionless. Inside the buildings, sweating flesh slept unsuspecting. No longer a trace of struggle. Yet the stench of war still hung in the air, an oppressive fog. Or was she imagining it, had she imagined it before as well? Did that crowd driven by fear exist only in her mind? She ran faster. Kopenhagener Strasse, Milastrasse. At the Cantian Stadium she saw police emergency squadcars on the sidewalk alongside ambulances. The fences around the stadium had been torn down. She heard muted voices from somewhere, then the cry: Over here. She ran to Eberswalder Strasse. Police cars barricaded the street. In front of them were men in uniform standing shoulder to shoulder. The shifting bodies of two policemen formed a break in the chain of cars, and Rosalind could see behind the barricade for two or three seconds. A headlight flooded the street with pale light and shone on the many bodies lying closely, one next to the other. Men and women in white gowns, civilians as well, were bent over them, but Rosalind could not make out what they were doing. At the entrance to the street, next to the emergency vehicles, men were building a wall that cut across the road and walkways from one building to the other. They placed one brick on top of the next without haste; the wall was already up to their hips. It's over, once again I've arrived too late, Rosalind thought. She knew how pointless the thought was because, as things were, the struggle she had wanted to take part in had not happened, not even for a second. It had already been decided in advance, which meant that it was out of the question to arrive in time. Keep moving, don't stop, away from here, keep going, a voice commanded. The gap between those in uniform closed and it wasn't until now, exposed to the police cameras, with the threatening voices still in her ear, that Rosalind understood what she had just seen. My God, she whispered. She walked in no given direction and hid in the shadow of a newsstand. It's as simple as that, one hundred twenty feet of wall, that's all you need. Eberswalder Strasse was divided in its western part from the bordering district of Wedding by the town wall. On both the northern and southern sides, five-storey buildings formed unbroken barriers. And now they were walling up the eastern entry. Or exit. In between were people, a thousand, two thousand, who knew how many. The next morning pedestrians rushing by would be amazed or note indifferently that where there had been a street the day before, there was now a wall. In a few weeks the wall will be covered with film posters and the call-up for those born in '68 to register for conscription. There used to be a street here, the people will recall, until that too fades into oblivion. Something has to be done, she thought, something ought to be done. Suddenly she heard a whispering pierce the silence, hissing voices from the air, as if the air itself were forming sentences.

It started in the stadium, they whispered.

No, at the border.

First at the stadium, then they walked to the border, a third voice whispered.

No, they wanted to go over the Wall immediately. I can see it from my window.

Nonsense. They wanted to get in from the West.

It started at the stadium, I tell you, they beat someone to death.

A building door opens nearby with a squeak, the whispering stops, windows are closed cautiously. Rosalind still hears muffled sounds from the amputated street, noises of objects thrown against one another, no more voices. There's nothing you could do, what good was it to anyone that she was standing here, she thought. At first hesitantly, then more determinedly, she left the scene of secret happenings. She ran and ran. Knaackstrasse, faster. Prenzlauer Allee. Keep going, don't stop. You couldn't do anything. Don't look back, Orpheus, Eurydice is following you, but don't look back. If I could only run faster. Steps, steps, fall in the next yard, the one after that, fall two thousand times, three thousand times. The flesh drags the bones until they can no more. To the train station, Martha, where can you escape to? Forwards is backwards. Every step a farewell. I have to pace off what I want to say farewell to. Days step out of the buildings alone and in groups, tired, serious, exhuberant, overslept, drunken days. They stand in the streets looking at me. Winsstrasse, I lived there once; was that twenty, thirty years ago? The years stand in the doorway and wave goodbye. I wave in return, invite them to come along with me. You belong to me, you were my years. They sadly shake their heads and slowly walk back into the building. Traitors, cowards, I'll go without you then, the trap door in my right temple for you as well: into oblivion with you all. Backwards is forwards. And you, Bruno?

The bar was almost empty now. Only Bruno and the Count were still sitting at the bar. The Count was sleeping with his brow resting on his forearm. His sparse strands of hair, which he usually combed elaborately from his left ear over his bald head to his right ear, now hung long over his shoulders. He was snoring quietly. The innkeeper, too, a chubby man with white eyelashes in a pink face, was asleep next to the radio, which droned golden oldies. Please, don't look at me like that, you're perfectly aware that I can...Bruno lifted his head with difficulty and looked around in search. The pupil of his right eye had gotten lost under his eyelid. Who's calling for me? Bruno said.

Me, Rosalind said.

Bruno let his chin fall back on his chest: And I thought he had come after all, but he's not coming, the scoundrel, but he knows I'm waiting for him, he has to know it, 'cause he has this...you know, this...wake up, Count. Bruno roughly shook the Count's shoulder, wake up, I forget his name.

With a fearful cry, the Count sat bolt upright, so violently that he almost fell off the long-legged bar stool.

What's his name, you know who I'm talking about, Bruno said, the one I'm waiting for 'cause he knows all that, everything.

The Count groaned. I had a horrible dream, awful, but I've already forgotten the details, he said carefully, laid his strands of hair back and flattened them firmly to his scalp with the flat of his hand.

What's this guy's name? Bruno said.

The Count straightened his bow tie with the silver stars.

You mean the Laplacean demon, Brünoh.

Right, Bruno cried, relieved, because there's this Laplacean demon who knows everything. Can you imagine that, Rosa? No, no, you can't. But, anyway, he knows it. Everything. He knows every tiny wheel that turns on the earth, he knows.

We've been waiting for him for twenty-two years, isn't that right, Brünoh?

Twenty-two years, Bruno said, do you know how to tap beer, Rosa?

Rosalind went to the bar, rinsed out two glasses and carefully filled them with beer.

To Laplace, Bruno said.

To the demon, said the Count.

Rosalind remained silent. She thought she had heard the

name Laplace somewhere before. He must have been a Marquis, Marquis de la Place, or was she mixing him up with the Marquis de Sade, no, de la Place, she had already heard of him, a philosopher, that is, but she didn't have the vaguest idea, not the foggiest, what he had to do with this demon who apparently knew everything and which Bruno and the Count had suddenly conjured out of their pockets.

Let's be patient then, the Count said. One night he'll come up to us and enlighten us, Brünoh, about the future too.

Which we'll no longer have, Bruno said. They laughed.

And about the past, the Count said.

Which is still our future, Bruno said. Delighted at their own banter, they laughed louder.

So we understand everything, Brünoh, the Count squeaked in exhuberance.

And turn over in our graves to boot, Bruno finished.

They shook with laughter so much that beer ran out of Bruno's nostrils, and the Count would finally have fallen off his stool if Bruno hadn't been holding him by the arm. Between sighs, groans and sneezes the pair's seizure gradually subsided. Bruno swished the dregs of his glass and followed with difficulty the circular motion of the bubbles. The Count accompanied the singer on the radio with a voice full of longing:...*ziehen die Fischer mit ihren Booten aufs Meer hinaus*...

I want to say goodbye, Rosalind said.

Do you hear that, Count, Rosa is leaving us.

The Count interrupted his singing. We'll miss you, Madame Rosalie, he said and continued singing...*bella, bella, bella Marie, bleib mir treu*...

Fair is the talk of men at sunset, Bruno declaimed, do you understand this female activism, Count?

I'm going now, Rosalind said. She hoped Bruno would

ask her something: So where do you want to go, Rosa, where do you hope to find what no one has ever found? But Bruno let his gaze float on the flat beer like fat roundels atop a broth, and asked nothing.

...*Marie, vergiss mich nie*, the Count sang.

*

She turned right at Kniprodestrasse. The shortest way to the train station was through the park. She avoided the well-lit and paved main paths, stuck to the narrow walkways, trying not to lose her direction. Everything seemed odd. The park was a barren wilderness, the cold was eternal. Memories of strollers, screeching children, sun-thirsty old women came from another life. It was a hundred years ago that these trees bore leaves. Only another twenty or thirty minutes to the train station. Through the rhythm of her steps she heard over and over ...*and my tribe are those Asra who die when they love*; this too was from another life. She had been sixteen or seventeen when she used to repeat it, again and again, in front of a mirror, looking into her eyes as though making a promise...*who die when they love*. Oh, how often she would have had to die. Or had she died; was the one who had sworn this oath long since dead, and have I spent my life like one who wasn't born to it? The line disappeared in the labyrinth of my forgetfulness from which it had just emerged.

A noise startled her, a plaintive sound like the groaning of a tree bent by the wind, or the melody of the Eolian harp, and yet it was most like a human sigh. Rosalind stood still and waited until it came again. Very quietly, a second trembling sigh followed, as if it were the faraway echo of the first. Rosalind followed it into the dense shrubbery and stayed there until renewed groaning showed her the way through the darkness. Underneath a broad maple tree she found a crouched figure who, with both arms clasped around his knees, was rhythmically rocking the upper part of his body, letting out the plaintive sound that had attracted her. She approached the figure silently and sat down at a distance of six or seven feet from it without being noticed. Rosalind was able to make out a man under the tree despite the darkness, he swayed as if in a trance, enclosed in his own embrace. It wasn't until she spoke to him, please don't be startled, she whispered, that he winced, but then said with a calm, almost unmoved voice: Ah, the time has come. I thought I still had some time. Let's go. He stood up slowly, and Rosalind saw that he was tall and powerfully built. She couldn't make out his face, but his voice, while very serious, sounded like that of a young man not older than thirty.

I don't know where you want to go, Rosalind said, but I have nothing to do with it.

I see, the man said and sat down again, that's nice.

He seemed to pay no attention to Rosalind's presence. He put his arms around his body as he had done before and let himself rock again. Every so often he let out one of the painful sounds he seemed to create by rocking and which pierced Rosalind's heart.

I don't want to come too close to you, Rosalind said, but may I ask you who you are and why you're sitting here in the cold?

It isn't cold, the man said. You have to relax, don't breathe too deeply, nor too shallow, and you'll find that your body adjusts. I'm sitting here because I have leave. I…I…I'm forbidden to talk to people, but I'm somewhat decompensated today. That must have escaped the professor's notice or else he wouldn't have given me leave.

Do you live in a clinic? Rosalind asked.

Oh yes, the man said, it's very nice, and I feel very good, very good, I feel very good, very good, I feel very good, very good, I feel...

That's all right, Rosalind said and reached for the man's hand, what's your name?

k 239.

That's your patient number, but what's your name?

Your hand is cold, the man said, you have to relax, don't breathe too deeply, but not too shallow either.

My name is Rosalind Polkowski.

Very glad to meet you, the man k 239 said. I'm only telling you this because I'm somewhat decompensated today. I'm not allowed to talk to people.

Rosalind asked herself whom the man wanted to talk to if not with people, and why he pronounced the word people as if it meant something strange, something forbidden. He had stopped swinging, and was nervously rummaging in the rustling shrubbery instead. He then fell silent. Several times he took a deep breath; Rosalind thought he was gathering breath for an important sentence which would explain his odd nocturnal doings, but he exhaled the air as heavily as he had sucked it in, and remained silent. Rosalind, discouraged by the man's monotonous answers, stopped asking questions. So they sat there divided and united by the stillness and darkness, next to each other. Then, either moved by his loneliness or overwhelmed by his distress, the man began to speak:

I am a clone, if you know what that is. A clone is, so to speak, a plagiarized original. While the mother of my original was in the third month of her pregnancy they removed a fetus

147

cell during a routine check-up unobserved, impreganated an egg with it and created me. Three months after my original was born, I was ready to leave the incubator where I had been allowed to grow. Since that day I have been serving science. I am proud to serve science. While I know my original well—one of my tasks is to simulate all aspects of his life—he has no inkling of my existence, although it is only thanks to me that he has his extraordinary career. I resemble him in every nerve fiber, in every cilium, in every talent. I am his mono-ovary twin. A large-scale scientific research project is being written about us: the development of the personality under real and clinical conditions. Being a well known personality and under constant medical monitoring, my original does his part as well without being aware of it. You may not believe this, but I chose his wife for him. I was shown two hundred women and my body functions were monitored electronically. The candidate I reacted most positively to was, how shall I put it, passed on to him surreptitiously. We thereby saved him from what might have been an unhappy marriage. That would have been far too great a risk, especially in light of the career prospects awaiting him. Isn't that wonderful?

And you, Rosalind said, you are a human being too, aren't you?

The man interrupted her. Oh no, you still don't understand. Theoretically I am a man, in reality I am a virtual copy of a human being, his shadow made flesh. The original, with his name and identity card, is the human being and lives his life; I am his control, that is my significance. For science, which I have been serving since the first day of my life, I am more important than the original. You see, that is the point of my existence.

But you liked the woman too, didn't you? Rosalind said.

Yes, very much, the man said, I still like her, which leads to the conclusion that he still likes her too, for I live with her just as much as he does. He lives with the original as befits him and I with the clone.

For ten years, since she had seen a film in which the earth with its inhabitants was only the electronic reflection of a seemingly real but in its turn another merely reflected earth, Rosalind had not been able to escape the sense of a strange, incomprehensible design. She was repeatedly assailed by the idea that she lived in a laboratory in which human protest was tolerated only so long as it was of use to behavioral science. Anyone who knew too much was destroyed. Why else were there so many people who matured and died so young? They had turned out too smart for their breeders and were able to piece together the hidden pattern of things. Madness and the capacity for suicide were cunningly conceived and the mechanisms implanted in people so as to block the final path to knowledge. Perhaps Clairchen had come closer to the secret than any of them in her insatiable desire for love, closer even than Martha. So close that the mechanisms began to function, to cause intolerable pain, and had finally given her the order to destroy herself. The longer Rosalind pursued the thought the deeper she was sucked into it. Life seemed to fit the model: the most disparate races, the climatic zones, epidemics and famines, the incurable diseases, once perceived as test programs and laboratory experiments, revealed to Rosalind a meaning not otherwise found in their brutal arbitrariness. Even the wars no one wanted and yet took place could be explained, if something unknown, obeying a reason of its own, ruled over mankind. Humanity was condemned to defend itself with the wrong means, because they were not allowed to learn the meaning of their existence. Her observation dissolved her store of the knowledge of life and left her unable to cope with the incomprehensible futility from which, up until that morning four nights earlier, she had thought to escape by holding on to reality. Now when her nightmare had become flesh, a human being sitting across from her who claimed to be no human being but a control for an experiment, reality remained silent. No rebellion, no horror, no disgust; a warm numbness coursed haltingly through her veins like clotting blood. So it was true, she thought, so it was true after all, while the man told how many liters of vodka he had had to drink to track down the causes for his original's bad decisions. The culprit is almost always alcohol when he makes mistakes, the man said. Consumption of alcohol, especially high-proof alcohol, makes us inclined to extreme unpredictability. You mustn't, please, imagine my task to be all that easy. His and my psychic conditions are identical only in their heredity, but not in their development. We were subjected, as you can imagine, to very different influences. Although they tried to reproduce his experiences in me using films, tape recordings, even drugs, the lack of immediacy could be compensated for only in part. In order to achieve real simulation—and you will understand now why even the most sensitive of machines cannot replace a clone—my imagination was needed.

The longer he spoke, the more the man's anxiety gave way to an oppressively euphoric rapture. His voice rose, forced into a shriller register. His mouth seemed unable to articulate sentences as fast as he wanted to utter them. The words pushed and shoved each other along the narrow track of his voice; now and again one fell down and went head over heels

150

with a shrill cry.

You'll have to admit, the man continued in haste, that I live an unusually rich life. I say this although I know that I don't deserve the word life. But in a certain sense I have a life, in that I reconstruct his life. At the same time—and with my total consent—I fulfill my duty to science, which enables me to know my original better than he could ever know himself. While he is subject to his desires and lusts, I have learned, if only out of necessity, to draw sustenance entirely from my mind. My body serves me as a tool for perception; and I elicit feelings for the purpose of deeper insight into my original. Each of my insights into his behavior enters into his program for psychosomatic perception. I surround him, investigate his most secret drives, which then can be either used or allowed to atrophy according to their importance for his future. Do you understand what that means? He moved closer to Rosalind, who felt violent disgust at the idea that he might touch her or even, in the enthusiasm with which he spoke, spray her face with saliva.

Do you recognize the truth? the man asked.

Before, when I met you, you were sad, Rosalind said. You called that decompensation.

Oh, you do not recognize the truth. How otherwise could you take your sympathy and pour it over me like fresh milk instead of grasping that it is me who could have pity? It depends on me how he will turn out. I am leading him; he follows me. I even decide his states of mind by finding out which of them help him to perform better, and which impede him. Thanks to my work, we know that every type of extreme emotion lessens his performance. His basic medical treatment—primarily with electrolytes and hormones—allows for short-term peaks during phases of vacillation or exhaustion. Without me he would be an ordinary man, a nothing, a nobody. Do you understand now?

Rosalind was shivering. A brisk wind had come up as if from a suddenly opened door. The cloud cover was torn here and there, and there were ice-grey scraps of sky visible through the branches of the maple tree. There are no strangers here anymore; two weeks before Martha disappeared she had said: no strangers, no secrets, only plagiarized copies. She had fled from her discovery; where to flee to, Martha, where? Don't you have any desire to live at all? Rosalind said, too softly for the man to have understood her.

You are not answering me, all right, remain silent, he said. But you are sure to be convinced by what I am about to confide in you. Should anything happen to my original, the man whispered, I have been equipped to take his place. No one knows which personalities of public life can be replaced at any time by clones; even we clones can only guess. Needless to say, every cosmonaut has a clone who is indispensible for maintaining secrecy in the case of a fatal accident. The clones of statesmen are used less often after fatalities than in the case of deviant behavior by their originals. In all known cases the performance of clones has greatly outstripped that of their originals. Clones are more dependable, less susceptible to breakdown; their lives are in the service of science. This is their guiding principle in life. If one day I have to replace my original—circumstances that I don't want to talk about now could make that possible—I will be able to demonstrate what a clone is really capable of.

The man's increasing excitement, his choppy and short-winded speech, the wild gestures he used for emphasis made him seem to be more and more of a madman. It was possible, after all, that nothing of what he had said was true.

Perhaps he was an aficionado of science fiction who had gone mad, for whom, one night, fear of the future had become the present in his confused brain. This is also why he had made such a tragic impression on her when she had first seen him. Somewhere in his scattered thoughts he still knew about the previous life that had robbed him of his reason. It had cost Rosalind her legs, but this poor man his mind. The man seemed to have thrown all caution to the wind. He had stood up and was shouting as though addressing hundreds of thousands of listeners and not Rosalind alone. Unsure whether she should feel compassion or disgust, she could only stare at his odd behavior.

The true performance of a prototype, he said, can never be tested on the original, but can be seen only in the clone. From an unbiased consideration one can easily deduce that the clone embodies the real, unadulterated original, whereas the supposed original is merely a random, often even pathological, deviant. The mind of Einstein need never have been lost to the world. Ten, twenty, a hundred true Einsteins, more real than the original, because unspoiled by life's contingencies, could simultaneously be achieving their works in science.

A geneticist gone mad, thought Rosalind, who was gradually becoming convinced of being in the presence of a mentally-ill person. The eternal dream of immortality, the man cried. In another two thousand years we will be able to show the geniuses of our day in the flesh to school children, the fiftieth or sixtieth copy of them, and still the unfaded originals.

An obsessed scientist who wanted to or was supposed to breed human clones, Rosalind thought, and later perfected his ghastly work on himself. That might be it. Rosalind found comfort in the justice of her second assumption. That's how it must have been, she thought: he's gone mad in despair at not being able to breed a human clone, and he has become his own clone. They have confined him to a clinic which he ran away from tonight.

The best thing to do would be to take him back to the clinic. They would have discovered him missing by now. Who knows what might happen to him if he goes around the city telling his horror stories. The police might arrest him for divulging public secrets or for slandering the state. There was no telling what sort of international incident this could lead to if the man were to meet a foreigner, or worse, a journalist. The secret services of the world might be destabilized for years. This prospect was more a source of satisfaction than concern to Rosalind, and only the disturbed man's defenselessness prevented her from letting things take their natural course.

Should I see you back to the clinic? she asked him, trying to suppress the pity in her voice.

That won't be necessary, he said, obviously irritated at his lecture being so rudely interrupted. He had just introduced the problem of impending overpopulation as the result of the increased cloning of valuable genetic material. They will pick me up before long, I already hear steps, he said and brushed the leaves from his trousers. An instant later the bushes opened, and a not particularly tall woman stepped over the shrubbery.

It is time, she said.

The man pointed at Rosalind and said: We have to take her along, I've told her everything. Both of them stepped toward Rosalind, and when they came within an arm's length of her, Rosalind opened her eyes. She saw, very close, her own face; the powerful fingers that were already grasping for her belonged to a woman who wore her face. The man next to her looked like Robert Redford or the interrogator who resembled him. Don't touch me, Rosalind screamed, back, back, go away! She was still screaming when the two had long since faded into the shadows of the first morning light.

I fall exhausted onto the damp leaves. Images cross one another, trees, a window, white walls, my face on a strange woman; and, over and over again, Ida—Ida in the dark velvet dress with the white lace collar hand in hand with the young man named Hans; Ida with the encrusted cavity where her mouth used to be; Ida crying with the carpet beater in her hands, her lips forming a word, but I don't understand it. And over everything the rotting smell of dying autumn. Death. Are you here, I say, and no one answers. I forget. I distinctly feel the reel in my head rewinding with no effort on my part, and without my being able to stop it. I try to remember where I am, but I don't know anymore, I have only one sentence left: I have to go to the train station. The train station is everywhere, someone says, or I say it, for I know the voice like my own. The train station is everywhere, the voice says again, and now I know for sure that it was me who spoke although it is not my voice. I lift my head and at the same time press my eyelids firmly together because the sun is glistening around me as in the desert. My fingers, thin childlike fingers, feel the stones I am lying on. My eyes find it hard to get used to the light. Not far away I see sleeping men and women like myself, stretched out in the narrow shadow of the buildings. Their heads are pillowed on plastic bags containing everything they own. I have the same sort of bag next to me. On the other side, under the scaffolding, someone has furnished a living room: a filthy, ripped-up sofa, chairs without legs, a vegetable crate. Three men and a woman—I know them all—pass a liquor bottle around. I wave to them. Hey, Martha, come over here, they call. I sit up, I feel sick, and my hands are shaking, but I remember now. The cracked building walls, the windows either nailed shut or broken, the garbage thrown about by the wind, the sweetish smell of refuse like a rotting field of rape, the name on the street sign: The Bowery.

I came here from Spain, Algiers and Toronto. I want to stand up to go to my friends on the other side, who are still calling for me, but I'm too weak. I can't manage to get up on my legs, which are trembling no less than my hands. A woman comes up to me. I approach her and ask her to help me. She is neatly dressed and her hands are not trembling, she is going for a walk in this, my street. All the same I say to her, help me please. She wants to continue walking and I recognize her instantly. Rosalind, I say, Rosalind Polkowski. She stands still. She searches me helplessly with her eyes until they finally light up with the expected start of recognition. Martha, are you Martha? she asks. Instead of helping me up, she sits down next to me and cries. I have been looking for you, she says.

You've found me now, I say.

Her gaze is a mirror in which I can recognize my grey, unclean skin, my feverish eyes, the cracked scarred lips, the dirty hair, the rotten teeth. Her horror disgusts me although at the same time I have the impression I'm looking at myself with these frightened eyes. Or am I Rosalind; or am I a third person?

Martha straightened herself up. Stop screaming, she said.

That's why, Rosalind whispered, that's why.

What do you mean, that's why?

That's why you left.

Do you have a cigarette? Martha asked.

They smoked. They sat next to each other and didn't exchange looks anymore. What did you expect, Martha said, a husband in a custom-tailored suit, or in jeans and a beard—same difference these days—two gifted children, that sort of thing?

I don't know, Rosalind said, nothing particular, but not this.

I have to puke, Martha said. She bent over to one side and vomited bilious phlegm against the building. It's due to inflation, she said. As the professor once said, the rising cost of time takes half of our lives, by now it's probably more. You don't get anything anymore for hours or days; the minutes you can forget altogether. Every special experience has to be paid for with years or decades. If you're stingy with time, you get nothing at all, at best miserable plagiarisms. If you think you can save the years and pay in days and weeks, like your grandmother did when she was young, you'll end up having pointlessly wasted your time. I have spent almost everything. I know you think it was only ten years, but I paid forty for it, or fifty.

I gave ten and got one, Rosalind said, because one was like the others.

What is a year, said Martha, it's like an empty cardboard box. Time counts in experiences and not in years.

The sweat streamed from Rosalind's pores, evaporated into the steamy air, melted the border between her body and everything surrounding her. She was menaced by a feeling of disintegration. She looked over at Martha, who lay dully on the wall, her eyes half covered by her heavy eyelids. She had to think of Georg and his version: you drove her out.

She timidly caressed Martha's hand. Did I drive you out? she asked. Martha smiled without opening her eyes. There's no answer to that, Rosalind, I was looking for something.

Did you find it?

No, Martha said, but I looked for it with all my strength. Do you know, you have to find the least useful part of yourself and chrerish it, that's the beginning of your biography, the professor said. Do you remember?

You wanted to find your father.

Martha laughed her snickering, secretive laugh. My father is an insignificant policeman in Berlin. Didn't I ever tell you that? The word doesn't exist for what I'm searching for. I could call it apple or pyramid or tree, it wouldn't make any difference. Every person carries within them the image of what they have to seek, everyone has a different image, and it's impossible to think up a word to carry all these images. I once thought that I had found what I was looking for. I was walking along a country road between two towns. I don't know anymore which ones. It was summer. Suddenly, the sky darkened until it was black, a wind rose, and the first raindrops fell like pin pricks. I went under a tree, but soon the rain was so heavy that it fell through the dusty leaves and ran onto me in grey rivulets. I went back to the road, where the rain streamed on me, and within a few seconds not an inch of me was dry. Once wet, I lost my disgust. Instead of resisting the inevitable I abandoned myself to it, indifferently at first, but then with excitement. The water washed around me like the sea, it flowed into my eyes, into my ears, it flowed from my hair onto my neck, across my back, it stuck my dress to my body like skin. I opened my mouth and let the water flow into me. I then fell or threw myself to the ground intentionally, wallowed in the mud, I felt my heart grow and grow, and for a moment I thought I was even the rain and the earth, violently united. Half an hour later everything was over. Wind and clouds had disappeared over the horizon like wild horsemen. Clouds of steam rose from the ground and began the cycle anew. My hair and my dress dried, I rubbed the bits of encrusted mud from my skin. An unknown harmony sounded within me like a miraculous chord, as though I myself were an instrument and something had plucked all the strings so artfully that no single tone interrupted the rapture of the moment. I know something since then.

A group of young people with quite small pug noses and almond-shaped eyes walked past. They were talking in a language that Rosalind could not understand, but which seemed familiar to her. They were carrying peculiar objects—large painted cardboard walls, long poles, one of them was dragging a wooden staircase painted white. They walked fast in spite of the heat, as though toward a destination. Their childlike and cheerful faces, Rosalind thought, did not belong to this street in which everything, even the cars parked at the roadside, looked squalid.

Did you find something? Martha called to them.

Not yet, but we'll manage, they called back without stopping.

A theater troupe from Alaska, Martha explained. Eskimos who played *Antigone* here in the city, very close by. They were a success. One day the grandfather of the leading actress died, and all the members of the troupe went home to bury him. When they came back their theater had been sold, and shortly afterwards was torn down by the new owner. They've been walking around for weeks now looking for a new building in which to play. They at least know what they're

159

looking for, Rosalind said. I looked for you, I've found you and what's the better for it?

Martha waved me off impatiently. You looked for me as little as I did for my father. You hoped I could tell you what you really want.

Rosalind kept silent.

And now you're disappointed because you don't know, Martha said. She reached for her plastic bag and stood up slowly, supporting herself on Rosalind's shoulder. You are too afraid, Rosalind, she said, stupid, childish fear, which to make matters worse you consider sensitivity. We are not immortal. Come along, we're going to see the others.

Martha takes my hand and pulls me along among the honking cars to the other side of the street where her friends greet us with a drunken howl. The two men are Harry and Billy. Billy is black and young. Harry is white. The length and breadth of his face is furrowed with deep wrinkles. When he laughs he exposes his toothless jaws. In spite of the heat both of them are wearing colored knit caps on their heads. The woman, Vicky, unlike the men, looks as if she had just gotten out of the bath tub. She too owns three plastic bags filled to bursting, in which she rummages from time to time, to fish for a handkerchief, a mirror or lipstick. Harry hands Martha and me the liquor bottle, me first. I have to force myself to put the bottle to my mouth—it has just been on Harry's scabby lips. The liquor is revoltingly warm and burns my throat. My stomach twitches and presses the stuff back into my throat. I swallow it again, this time more gently. Cheap booze that quickly goes to my head. I lie down on the ground, Martha and the others talk in a language I can't understand. I can understand them only when they laugh. Martha's laughter is shrill and loud like I've never heard it before. I register the very different feelings that assault me together when passersby glance at us in contempt, pity, even fear. I am ashamed of lying here; I am ashamed of being ashamed. I don't give a good goddamn what these people with their glances think of me. I don't believe that I don't care. I despise these people with their glances who don't fear anything except that but for the grace of God, go I. I feel pity for those who are so frightened, the way I am now afraid, but I have put that behind me. The worst is yet to come. I want to hide and stretch myself out voluptuously in the stinking dust of the street. I would like to laugh as raucously as Martha. I laugh, I screech like a she-monkey. I'm sick of being clean and walking among people neatly dressed. I stand up, pull down my drawers and piss in the middle of the sidewalk. I scream once again like a she-monkey and do not feel ashamed. I find myself disgusting; I like myself that way. Billy comes, attracted by my cries. We roll on the hard pavement. The people with the glances have to step over us or walk around us. I have closed my eyes and am buried beneath Billy's stench. Billy smells of liquor and a week of sweat. With his knees he presses my thighs apart, and we mate like animals. The stones scrape the skin from my flesh, my head beats on the pavement to Billy's rhythm, Billy's biting sweat seeps through my pores. Billy stands up and goes back to the others. I remain lying on the ground, a shadow buried in the stone. I don't exist anymore, I have nothing more to fear. I fall asleep in this position. When Martha wakes me up it is evening. A grey-white fog hangs over the city, and the midday heat still oozes from the heated walls. We are once again alone, Martha and I.

Where are the others? I ask.

What others, Martha says, come, get up, I want to show

you something. Beneath the pale evening light the street lies wretched and stained like the scene of a continuing struggle, whose victims lie hastily buried beneath the city trash. We turn into a sidestreet. Martha is walking fast with firm steps and her back ramrod straight. I have a hard time keeping up with her, remain a few steps behind. I know that I have been through this all once before. I have already walked over this torn-up asphalt past old buildings with crumbling plaster. Martha pushes open a heavy door. The stairwell is dark. We walk up to the second floor. Martha stops in front of a green iron door, takes a key out of her jacket pocket and opens the door, behind which, recognizable in the semidark only in outline, is a familiar room. Come. Come in, Martha says and chuckles secretively. Slowly, as if my senses first had to feel their way through a dream, I recognize the uncertain smells of the room, the four white walls, the furniture.

This is my room, I say, and no one answers me because Martha has long since disappeared, and Rosalind sat with her lame legs crossed, alone in her chair. A glance at the street showed the accustomed scene: the solid façades of the four-storey buildings with their high windows spreading indifference, built at the turn of the century, and, as it now seemed, for eternity. A thin-spun rain covered the dreary November morning with an icy sheen. It was, it is, it will be; time coiled up like snakes. And Rosalind found herself again, unawares. Well, here I am again, she thought, more bemused than surprised that her complicated efforts to leave her point of departure had brought her safely back to her own thoughts. So here I am once again, she said, and decided not to ask whether it was good or bad, whether her situation was evidence of strength or weakness, whether she had wanted this or its opposite.

162

Although all the furniture and objects were in their accustomed places, the room seemed different to her, narrower, more cramped, a feeling she could not explain. The proportions were still the same but her impression grew stronger. She saw everything faraway, shrunken in scale, as if viewed through the wrong end of a telescope. At the same time their scale created the illusion that these miniatures would reveal their true, unsuspected size the moment one came close to them. She tried to correct the image through memory; no use, any more than, once grown, she could ever change the scale of images recollected from her childhood.

From outside she heard the murmur of the swelling rain, which the wind lashed along the streets. Heavy drops spattered on the windowsill. The dry air in the room burned her skin and the sight of the clear, cold rainwater made her thirsty. To open one's mouth wide and let the water run in, to get wet, she thought, to be wet with the rain, yes, that would be fine.

About the translator: David Newton Marinelli translated Monika Maron's acclaimed first novel, *Flight of Ashes,* which Readers International published in 1986. Mr Marinelli has also translated works by Thomas Bernhard, Hermann Kant and Guido Gozzano. He obtained a Bachelor of Arts degree in history at Ohio State University and two Masters of Arts degrees at Rutgers University (New Jersey, USA). Since 1981 he has lived in Vienna, where he is completing his doctoral dissertation on the comic opera librettos of Carlo Goldoni.

Readers International (RI) publishes contemporary literature of quality from Latin America and the Caribbean, the Middle East, Africa, Asia, and Eastern and Central Europe.

If you would like to know more about **RI**'s publishing program, ask your local bookseller, or write to us for a catalogue:

Readers International
8 Strathray Gardens
London NW3 4NY
Great Britain

Readers International
P.O. Box 959
Columbia, LA 71418
USA